THE CLOUD OF UNKNOWING

STORIES BY **MIMI LIPSON**

COUNT STORE

yeti

3 1969 02250 6108

YETI books are published by Yeti Publishing LLC
and distributed to the trade by Verse Chorus Press
PO Box 14806, Portland OR 97293 | yetipublishing.com

Versions of these stories have appeared in the following magazines:
"Lou Schultz" in *Joyland*; "Moscow, 1968" in *Witness*; "The Cloud
of Unknowing" in *BOMB*; "The Breakfast Shift," "Catch of the Day,"
and "Garbage Head" in *YETI*; "The Smockey Bar" and "Safe,
Reliable, Courteous" in *Contrappasso*; "The Minivan" in *Chronogram*;
"Mothra" in *The Brooklyn Rail*; "the_lettuce" in *Harvard Review*.

ISBN 978-1-891241-59-8 (paperback)
ISBN 978-1-891241-95-6 (e-book)

Library of Congress Cataloging-in-Publication Data

Lipson, Mimi.
  [Short stories. Selections]
  The cloud of unknowing / stories by Mimi Lipson.
    pages cm
  ISBN 978-1-891241-59-8 (pbk.) -- ISBN 978-1-891241-95-6 (e-book)
1. Short stories, American. I. Title.
PS3612.I675C56 2014
813'.6--dc23
                              2013049085

PRAISE FOR *THE CLOUD OF UNKNOWING*

This is Lipson's classless utopia, in which even fools are suffered gladly so long as they are lively and authentic fools. Her language is clean, her observations clever and sure, and her protagonists generous of spirit. This wise, compassionate book is also a lot of fun to read.
—BONNIE JO CAMPBELL

Mimi Lipson writes in a plainsong, just-the-facts style that somehow delivers her footage in high definition. Her characters inhabit a world that is beneath them, a world in which they are stuck, with a lot of grace and stupidity. She is a master of making you very comfortable and secure, warm and cozy while she throws your shoes under the house and drives off in your car.
—GARY PANTER

"A scintillating collection of stories, full of well observed details. Mimi Lipson is a fabulous stylist."
—HA JIN

For Luc

Contents

THE SCHULTZ FAMILY

Lou Schultz

When Lou Schultz got to the Avis desk at the Orlando airport, the compact car he'd reserved was not available, nor was there a midsized left on the lot. They'd had no choice but to upgrade him straight to the top: a brand-new 1973 Chrysler Imperial, white with cream interior. He decided to let the kids believe that he'd splurged and was kicking off their holiday in style. Jonathan, ten, was splayed out in the backseat with a map he'd gotten at the rental desk, and seven-year-old Kitty, winner of the coin toss, sat up front next to Lou playing with the radio dial. The three of them were cruising under a pale Florida sky, en route to Villa Serena, a real estate development in Winter Haven. Lou had planned their vacation around the coupons and discounts he'd been promised in return for touring one of the model homes.

"Doesn't it sound grand, kids? *Vee-ya Serena.*"

The driver's seat of the Imperial was like an overstuffed recliner, so preposterously plush that he could bury his fist in the armrest, and the steering and brakes responded to his slightest touch. Looking down at the imitation-burl instrument panel, he saw that he was going fifteen miles over the speed limit without even trying. On the subway ride to the airport and all during the flight, Lou had felt a mounting irritation at the thought of five days in Florida—and particularly the two days at Disney World he had promised the kids—but his mood was lifting now that they were on the road. The week's theme, he decided, would be unapologetic leisure: motels, swimming pools, sunshine and Donald Duck. He'd brought along a mycology guide, and he even hoped to get in a little mushroom hunting.

Kitty at last found a station. A lugubrious male voice crooned over a bed of strings: "*I remember all my life / Raining down as cold as ice.*"

"Aaah! Barry Manilow!" Jonathan shouted. "Turn it off!"

"Ba-*ree* Ma-*nee*-loff. A Polish singer?"

"Dad!"

"I want to hear this Polish singer, this Maniloff." Unforgivable schmaltz, but having committed to the joke, he made them listen to the entire song.

Lou taught Slavic languages at Harvard, and every summer he took groups of tourists around the Balkans and the Soviet Union, ditching their Intourist guide and leading by improvisation. They drove all day in rented VW Microbuses and slept in army surplus tents. When Lou and his wife, Helena, separated a year earlier, one of her chief complaints was that she'd been left at home with the children for eight summers in a row. Lou hadn't taken her protests seriously until it was, perhaps, too late, but since she'd moved out, he'd discovered that he enjoyed spending time with his family.

Kitty leaned out her window watching the furniture showrooms and car lots roll past. "A Gilligan's Island tree! And another. Andanotherandanotherandanother," she chanted.

"It's like Ohio, only with palm trees," Jonathan said, looking up from his map.

"Sohio. You mean it looks like Sohio," Kitty said.

"Sorlando," he answered, picking up the thread. "Sorlando, Sflorida."

"Spine Hills," Kitty said. "Scocoa Beach. Daddy, are we going to Scocoa Beach?"

This was the Sohio Game, which Lou had regretted inventing ever since their trip to his sister's house in Akron a few years earlier. The game was named after the Sohio gas station chain, and there was only one moronically simple rule: add an 's' to any place name. Smassachussetts. Snew Hampshire. Scambridge, Smedford, Spittsburgh, on and on, ad nauseam.

"Let's play Three Thirds of a Ghost," he said, hoping to nip it in the bud. "I'm thinking of a word that starts with 'h'."

"'h' . . . 'a'," Jonathan said. "Kitty, it's your turn."

"'h', 'a', 'p'," Kitty said.

"'h', 'a', 'p' . . . 'a'."

Jonathan thought for a moment. "I challenge."

"Hapax!" Lou said, smiling into the rearview mirror. "One third of a ghost for Jonathan."

His son slumped angrily in his seat. "What's a hapax?"

"As in hapax legomenon. Remember, we were talking about hapax legomena yesterday?"

"Forget it," Jonathan said, picking up the map again. "I don't want to play."

After turning into a golf course by mistake, Lou found the entrance to Villa Serena. A prim decorative fence edged either side of the driveway, and a sign planted in the bright green lawn announced "Model Home Information." The only landscaping was a stand of date palms off to one side, shading nothing in particular. A cluster of low ranch houses ringed the parking lot, each with its own white gravel yard. Lou moored the Imperial in a space between two golf carts.

"Who's coming on the tour?" he asked. Kitty got out of the car, but the boy was still sulking.

The agent, an attractive woman in a white pantsuit, met them outside the sales office with a ring of keys. "Mr. Schultz?" She held out her hand. "Welcome to Villa Serena. I'm Marjorie Dale." Her smile stayed fixed as her eyes moved to Kitty and then back to Lou. "There are not a lot of children here, Mr. Schultz. In fact, most of the residents are retired. I think that's mentioned in our brochure?"

"You're never too young to retire!"

They followed Mrs. Dale around the model home, tactfully admiring the drapes and wall-to-wall carpets as she pointed them out. The living room was divided into two levels separated by a wrought iron railing. The "his and hers closets" in the "master bedroom," to which Mrs. Dale drew Lou's particular attention, had plastic bi-fold doors. In the kitchen, a florescent light fixture hummed over the no-wax floor.

"Mrs. Schultz would certainly appreciate the trash compactor, wouldn't she?" Lou winked at Kitty. "And she's been pestering me for a dishwasher, too."

Back at the office, Lou went over next week's lesson plan in his head, on Russian palatal mutations in the conjugation of –at stemmed verbs, while Mrs. Dale yammered on about "customization options." When she'd stopped talking, he filled out a travel voucher and collected his coupons, and they were back on the road in under an hour. He cocked his elbow out the window and relaxed into his pillowy seat, taking in the Cinescope view of shopping plazas and country clubs through the Imperial's wide windshield.

"So, what do you think of this car?" he asked Jonathan, who had switched places with his sister and was now up front. "Like riding on a cloud, isn't it?"

"Like floating on a marshmallow," Jonathan said, bouncing.

"What say we keep it?"

"Yeah!"

"How about you, Kit? What do you think of Daddy's new car?"

She was quiet for a minute. "I don't know."

"And what about that house, hah?" he said, warming up to the bit. "How would you like to live in a gracious new home at Villa Serena? We can all take up golf!"

Kitty turned her back to him and leaned on the package

shelf. "Can we call Mommy?"

"You just saw her this morning. Wouldn't you rather wait and call her when you have something to tell her?" Was it possible, he thought irritably, that she was already homesick?

Lou had a coupon for the El Morocco Motel. The sun was already low when they checked in and the day hadn't been warm, but Jonathan and Kitty were in the pool by the time Lou got out of his shower. He went outside and sat on a lounge chair in the astroturfed courtyard with a newspaper he'd taken from the lobby. First Jonathan, then Kitty climbed out and stood on the lip of the pool holding their noses. Jonathan counted one-two-three and they jumped, upright and stiff-legged, back into the water, then climbed out and jumped in again. The sun sank below the cement wall and the underwater lights came on, casting the children's faces in a cathode glow as they paddled back and forth.

Lou wished now that he'd tried harder to convince Helena to come with them to Florida, but she'd said she was too busy—substitute teaching, waitressing at a coffee shop. That was Helena: serious and self-sufficient. She'd refused his financial help when she moved out. Well, he hadn't explicitly offered any, but only because he knew she *would* refuse. And perhaps, a little, because he'd hoped she would become discouraged. Even exhausted, Helena was beautiful—as desirable as ever to him, perhaps more so. He had coaxed her into his—their—bed a few times over the past year, and he hadn't abandoned the idea that he might persuade her to give up her apartment and move back in.

The sky was completely dark when Kitty and Jonathan got out of the pool. They were shivering and their lips were blue, so he made them get into a hot shower. They ate dinner at the coffee shop next to the motel and went back to their room and played a few hands of gin rummy. Lou supervised the flossing and brushing, tucked the kids in, and turned off all the lights but the one on the nightstand between the two big beds.

"We're going to Disney World tomorrow, right?" asked Jonathan.

"Yes, tomorrow," Lou said. "Probably tomorrow. If not, then certainly the day after. Now, who is in the mood for a Comrade Borodin story?" he asked, removing his shoes and lying down on the other bed, arms folded behind his head. His mind was already working, and he didn't wait for a reply. "It seems that Comrade Borodin's wife, the beautiful Grushenka—"

"The countess?" interrupted Kitty. "The one who liked to catch flies in her mouth?"

"The *former* countess," Lou said, remembering that he'd used the name before. "She'd renounced her title, as Comrade Borodin considered the aristocracy to be decadent."

"Is there a hedgehog in the story?"

"As it happens, yes, there is a hedgehog. Borodin's best friend was a hedgehog named Chauncey. But more of that later. As you will recall, Comrade Borodin worked at the F. Gladkov Main Moscow State Institute of Physical Culture, which is sometimes called simply—"

"Glavmosgosfizkult," Jonathan said.

"Precisely. Glavmosgosfizkult. One summer, Comrade Borodin's brigade went to the Ural Mountains to construct a hydroelectric power station. In fact, Borodin's brigade had been called away every summer for eight years to some eastern province: a cement factory in Kamchatka one year, the next year a magnesium processing plant on Lake Baikal, and so forth."

"Dad?"

"Yes, Jonathan?"

"Next time you go to Russia, can I go with you?"

"Maybe so. Could be."

"Dad, what about Chauncey?" mumbled Kitty, already half asleep.

"That was what Grushenka wanted to know—what about Chauncey? Because during these summers, it fell to Grushenka to change Chauncey's litter box and take him for walks.

"'Dearest Chauncey,' Grushenka would say while they walked, for indeed they had become very close, 'why does Borodin prefer the companionship of his brigade?'

"'Ah, but you are wrong, Grushenka,' said the hedgehog. 'He thinks of you day and night, and even keeps your picture on his footlocker. It is well known that he gazes tenderly at your yellow hair and red cheeks before he falls asleep, so that he may dream of you, and that every day, as he mixes concrete for the foundation of the hydroelectric power station, he whispers the name *Grushenka*.'"

The sheets rustled as Jonathan turned on his side. Lou saw that they were both asleep now. They looked so much alike: the same sharp chins and messy, shoulder-length hair—as dark as his, but straight and fine as corn silk, like Helena's. Kitty had on her brother's old tiger-striped pajamas, the ones she'd worn for Halloween last fall. She'd invented a mythological creature with the pajamas and a rabbit-fur hat and a face mask of a mouse that she'd picked out at the drug store. As Lou undressed, switched out the light, and lay down again on his own bed, he thought about another story.

She was nineteen years old when they met, and already a graduate student at the University of Chicago, where she'd enrolled in the college at age fifteen. He was studying on the GI Bill. She'd been looking for a Russian tutor, and they'd given her his name at the department. She came to his basement apartment on Drexel Avenue—shy and quiet, a sylph in a peasant skirt. He told her to memorize Tatiana's letter to Onegin.

When she returned the next week, they sat on orange crates in his room, and she recited for him in halting Russian:

> I write this to you—what would one want?
> What else is there that I could say?
> 'Tis now, I know, within your will
> To punish me with scorn.
> But you, for my unhappy lot
> Keeping at least one drop of pity,
> You'll not abandon me.

In the morning they spread out Jonathan's map on the table in the coffee shop. "Look at this," Lou said, "we're only ten miles from Cypress Gardens!"

"But that's the opposite direction from Disney World," Jonathan said.

"I think we have a coupon for Cypress Gardens." He looked through his billfold. "Indeed we do; two free passes. We can leave Kitty in the car."

"Daddy!"

"All right, I guess I can pick this one up. You got the hockey tickets." Lou had been saying this for years. "You got the hockey tickets," he'd say as he put a dime in the turnstile or paid for their pizza or handed over their tickets at the movie theater.

"It's a garden, Daddy?" Kitty asked. "A flower garden?"

"Flowers of every hue. And Spanish moss."

"I don't want to look at moss!" Jonathan protested. "I thought we were going to Disney World today."

"Well, I don't think we should be too rigid. Let the wind take us where it will, right? *Drifting along with the tumbling tumbleweeds.*"

They spent all morning at Cypress Gardens. Actresses in antebellum dresses fanned themselves on rustic footbridges. They saw a waterskiing exhibition, and then Lou took a picture of the kids sitting on a bench on a carpet-covered platform in front of a painted plywood backdrop that said "Citrus Royalty." It all reminded Lou a bit of strolling the grounds in a faded European spa town: Marienbad, with an overlay of all-American bunkum.

Lou hoped they could find a cheap place for lunch, perhaps a roadside hamburger stand. But after driving for an hour, he gave up and pulled into the parking lot of the Seminole Diner, a sprawling new building clad in sheet metal and pebbled stone-face. Out of habit, he steered them to a booth that hadn't been cleared off yet and swiped a few onion rings off a plate before a scowling waitress snatched it away.

"Who's in the mood for a tuna sandwich? " he said.

Jonathan leaned his elbows on the table and scrutinized the menu. "I want a Monte Cristo."

"I don't think you'd like it," Lou said, hoping to redirect him to something less expensive. "They're usually made with tongue. Fried pig's tongue."

"That's not what it says here. 'Danish ham and cheese, served on French toast and dusted with powdered sugar.'"

"We could go back and forth on this all day. How about a tuna sandwich? That's what I'm having. What about you, Kitty? What looks good?"

"When can we call Mommy?" she asked.

"Why don't we wait a day or two and then call her when we have something interesting to tell her? Or you could write her a postcard. I'll bet she'd love that. Now, what do you want to eat?"

"Can I have French toast?"

"French toast it is."

"How come she gets to have French toast and I can't have a Monte Cristo?"

"For chrissake. Have a Monte Cristo, then."

Jonathan only picked at his sandwich when it arrived. While poring over the menu, he had overlooked the fact that it came with jelly, which he didn't like. Lou gave Jonathan his coleslaw and ate the rest of the Monte Cristo himself.

A few miles south of Interstate 4 they stopped at a filling station. While their gas was being pumped, Lou got out to see if he could find a better map.

"Dad," said Jonathan, who had followed him inside, "don't get mad, okay?"

"What is it?"

"You have to promise not to get mad first."

"All right, I promise. I promise I won't get mad."

"I'm hungry. Can you buy me these?" He held up a packet of neon-orange crackers.

Lou took the crackers from Jonathan and looked at the package. Milk solids, palm oil, monosodium glutamate. Junk. He sighed and handed them back. "You're really hungry?"

"Yes, really, I am. I'm really hungry."

Lou spotted a cardboard box next to the cash register filled with little paper sacks. He picked one up; the bottom half of the sack was transparent with grease.

"Boiled peanuts," the attendant said as the cash drawer sprang open. "Wife makes 'em."

"Boiled peanuts! Now that's something you won't find in Cambridge. Let's get a bag of boiled peanuts instead of these." He took the crackers out of Jonathan's hand and put them back. "Where's your sister?"

Kitty was standing in front of the soda machine with the door open, tugging at a bottle.

"Daddy, can I have an orange soda?" she asked.

Lou pretended not to hear her. She followed them back to the car with her fists jammed in the pockets of her windbreaker, dragging her sneakers along the pavement, and got in next to Lou. There was a dispute about whose turn it was to sit in front. Jonathan and Kitty had agreed to switch off at each stop, but they'd neglected to agree on what constituted a stop, and since it had only been twenty minutes since they left the Seminole Diner, Kitty didn't think the gas station should count. She put up a half-hearted fight before climbing over the seat.

As they pulled out of the station, Jonathan popped a boiled peanut in his mouth and spat it out the window. "Blekh. This tastes like a boiled *toe.*"

"God damn it, Jonathan. You want to come with me next summer, and you won't eat a bag of peanuts? What do you think we eat over there? French toast and orange soda? If you want to spend two months in the Soviet Union, you'd better be prepared to live on cabbage soup and black bread."

Jonathan stared ahead angrily, clutching the greasy bag in both hands.

"It's all right," Lou said after a bit. "Pass them over here." He tossed a handful of peanuts into his mouth. It actually was a little like chewing on boiled toes. He swallowed the mouthful and put the bag down on the console.

He heard a sniffle from the back seat.

"Kitty, you can switch with Jonathan after the next stop," he said.

"I don't care."

"Are you mad at Daddy about the orange soda?"

"You said we were going to call Mommy."

"I said we could call her in a few days, Kitty. We can't be calling Mommy every time you get mad."

She threw herself down on the seat and began crying in earnest—howling sobs that Lou couldn't ignore. He pulled onto the shoulder, got out of the car, walked around, and opened the back door. She was curled up with her face buried in the seat back. "Why don't we go for a walk, Kitty?" He held out his hand for her. "Let's stretch our legs." Kitty climbed out, and they walked along the road for a bit. The sun had finally broken through, and bits of crushed shell glinted in the light-colored gravel. On both sides of the road were orange groves behind high page wire fencing.

"Daddy, I don't want to live in Florida," Kitty said when she'd calmed down. "Mommy won't like that house, and I want to stay in Cambridge with Mommy."

"Oh, Kitty. That was a joke."

"We were tricking the lady?" She looked up at Lou. Her face, blotchy from crying, still registered uncertainty.

"We were tricking the lady. We're going to Disney World, and maybe we're going to see the ocean, and then we'll get on a plane and go back to Cambridge."

"We aren't keeping the car?"

"Of course not! That was a joke, too. We'll ride our bikes when we get home, just like always."

He took her hand and they started walking back.

"Bold paynits," she said after a moment.

"What, honey?"

"Bold paynits. That's what the man called them."

"Oh," Lou said, "Boiled peanuts! What we've got here is a failure to commun'cate," he said, doing his best George Kennedy impression.

"What we *got* here is a failure to comm*un*'cate!" she answered. Then after a bit, "Daddy?"

"Yes, sweetheart?"

"Can I have an orange soda?"

"Yech. Why do you want an orange soda? It rots your teeth and makes you stupid. We're in the land of sunshine and oranges, Kitty. Why have a cheap imitation when you could have the real thing? There's no greater pleasure in life than biting into a piece of fruit that was just picked off a tree."

As he was saying this, he noticed a place near a fencepost where the bottom of the page wire fence had been bent back. He knelt down, looked around him, and tugged at it a little.

"And if it's not your tree," he said, standing back up, "so much the better!"

Lou pulled up alongside the spot where the fence was loose. Behind the cover of the Imperial, Jonathan slipped under with no problem. The back pocket of Kitty's pants snagged on a piece of page wire, but Lou freed it without tearing the corduroy too much, and she slithered the rest of the way through.

"Scoot!" he said when they were both inside. "Get away from the road so they can't see you. No, Kitty, leave the ones on the ground. We don't want those; we want fruit right off the tree."

They ran a few rows into the orchard. Jonathan could reach the oranges on the lower branches easily, but Kitty sprang up like a kangaroo again and again, grabbing at the air.

"The ripe ones are higher up," Lou shouted. "Jonathan, give your sister a boost so she can climb up there." Jonathan kneeled down and made a stirrup with his hands. Just as Kitty put her foot in it, Lou heard a tractor start up somewhere nearby. He whistled and waved them back.

As his children ran toward him, stolen oranges gathered up in their T-shirts, he wished with all his heart that he had not promised to take them to Disney World.

Lou had the first premonition of a headache the next morning as the Imperial passed under the Walt Disney World archway and entered the buffer zone surrounding the Magic Kingdom. A three-lane road funneled them into a vast outdoor parking lot. They boarded an open-sided shuttle that dropped them at the ticket office, where the line zigzagged through what seemed like a quarter mile of roped stanchions. When they got to the front, Lou paid their admission and traded his Villa Serena coupon for a booklet of color-coded ride tickets and a map of the park.

"It looks like Purity Supreme money," Kitty said.

"What, honey?"

"She means food stamps," Jonathan explained.

"Can I hold them?" Kitty pleaded.

"Don't let her, Dad. She'll lose them. Give them to me."

Lou decreed that Kitty would hold the ticket book, keeping it in a zippered pocket, and Jonathan would hold the map, and after lunch they would switch.

It turned out they were still nowhere near the Magic Kingdom, which lay beyond a vast manmade lagoon and was accessible only by ferry. Lou had to admire this feat of land-gobbling showmanship; still, his stomach clenched with dread as he followed his children up the ramp. On board, he sat on a bench and watched the dock disappear, along with any hope of a quick get-away. Jonathan sat next to him studying the map. "That's Blackbeard's Island," he said, pointing into the glare. Kitty joined the crowd leaning over the rail. A shout went up when land appeared.

The first thing they saw when they disembarked was a cheery replica of a Victorian railroad station, high up on a landscaped embankment. Lou was momentarily dismayed, thinking that yet another leg of the journey awaited them, but Kitty and Jonathan pulled him into the stream of parents and children that flowed through a tunnel under the railroad trestle and into a bank of turnstiles, where Jonathan took the entry passes from Lou and handed them to the ticket-taker.

They found themselves in a simulacrum of small-town

America circa 1890, complete with a three-quarter-scale town hall built in an imitation of the Second Empire style. Covered arcades lined rows of old-timey storefronts. Everything was freshly painted in candy colors, and atop each mansard roof an American flag rippled in the mild breeze. They stood for a moment staring up the wide boulevard, immaculately paved and lined with saplings, at the bright blue Gothic spires of Cinderella's Castle.

"Come *on*!" Kitty said, leading the way.

Lou's headache was upon him fully now, and he was suddenly exhausted. The all-encompassing artificiality of his surroundings made everything seem foreshortened, so that he couldn't judge how far away the castle was. He followed Jonathan's blue windbreaker and Kitty's red one up the teeming sidewalk until they came to a gazebo, where he sat down and called out for them to wait. While he rested, Kitty and Jonathan hunched over the map. They seemed to have instantly gotten the lay of the land.

"Can we go on Cinderella's Golden Carrousel, Daddy?" Kitty asked.

"But the Frontierland Shootin' Gallery is on the way," Jonathan said. "Can't we go there first?"

Lou took the map. "I'll tell you what. I'm going to have a little lie-down over here." He pointed to a grove of cartoon trees behind a building in Tomorrowland that looked like a flying saucer. "You kids have fun, and come get me when you're ready for lunch." He handed the map to Jonathan. "Kitty, you still have those tickets, right?" She unzipped her pocket and took the booklet out and waved it.

Lou walked back the way they'd come. He found an alley, hidden from view by an information booth, which led to an open area. He saw the flying saucer building in the distance, and cut due southeast until he found the grove—in reality just a scattering of spindly young pines — where he stretched out on the grass and shut his eyes.

"Sir? *Sir*, are you awake?"

Two security guards stood over Lou. They were wearing short-sleeved uniforms with white Panama hats, and red ties patterned with tiny Mickey Mouse heads. Both of them were young and fit. The one who addressed Lou had a moustache. He looked a bit like Lee Van Cleef.

"Sir, is your name Mr. Schultz?"

"Yes, that's me. Lou Schultz," he said, sitting up. "How did you know my name?"

"We have your children, sir. They're waiting at the security office."

The guards escorted Lou back to Main Street, to a storefront between a candy shop and a photography studio. "Town Sheriff" was painted in ornate gold letters on the front window. Jonathan and Kitty were inside, sitting close together on a wooden bench.

The guard with the moustache kneeled down in front of them. "Is this man your father?" he asked.

"*Yes*," Jonathan said impatiently. "Dad, tell him we don't need a babysitter."

"What are you doing here?" Lou asked. "I thought you were going to Frontiertown."

"Frontierland," Jonathan said.

"Sir, we found your children in the park unattended."

"Ah! There's been a misunderstanding," Lou said. "They were not unattended. You see, they came here with me. But I thank you for your concern."

"I realize that, sir, but they were unattended when we found them."

"Yes, but we had plans to meet for lunch." He looked at his watch and saw that it wasn't even noon yet. "I suppose we might as well eat now."

"Mr. Schultz, your children were found taking coins out of the Cinderella Fountain."

Lou saw that their pants were soaked up to their knees. He furrowed his brow. "Is this true, children, what the officer is saying?" he asked, making his voice deep with concern.

"Kitty lost the tickets," Jonathan said. "She got to go on the Dumbo ride, and then we were supposed to go on 20,000 Leagues Under the Sea, but she lost all the tickets. The whole book. We were going to buy another ticket book."

"My pocket came unzipped," Kitty protested.

To Lou's relief, Kitty and Jonathan's outrage at getting picked up by security seemed to have preempted any complaints they might have had about spending under two hours at Disney World.

"Well kids," he said as the ferry nosed out into the lagoon, "what did you think of the Magic Kingdom?"

"So-called Magic Kingdom," Jonathan said.

"They acted like we were *babies*," Kitty said.

"Did they get all the coins off you?"

"Yeah, and fifty cents of it was mine," Jonathan said. "I found it in the back seat."

"Tell you what. Let's go to the beach and have a picnic lunch."

Resort hotels in various stages of completion lined the highway along the ocean. Lou stopped at a market a few miles north of Palm Coast and bought a loaf of bread and a jar of pickles and two cans of sardines. He asked the clerk where they could go swimming.

"Most of the beaches around here are private, but if you want to leave your car here, y'all can walk up the road a bit to the town boat launch," he said.

"Say, is there a payphone around here?"

"Out front, left of the door."

Lou got two dollars in change from the clerk and stuffed a dollar in a jar on the counter that had a picture of a kid in a leg brace taped to it.

"Much obliged," he said. "C'mon, kids," he called to Kitty and Jonathan, who were browsing a rack of comic books. "Who wants to talk to Mommy?"

"I do," yelled Kitty, but Jonathan was impatient to get to the water.

"The boat launch should be just up that way." Lou pointed north. "Go ahead and find us a spot."

Kitty talked to Helena while Lou emptied his flight bag and packed it with motel towels and their swimsuits and a few oranges. Kitty handed him the phone when he came back. "I'm gonna go find Jonathan, okay?"

Lou waved her off. "Careful crossing the street," he said. "Helena?"

"Hi, Lou."

"The kids are having a great time."

"They didn't mind getting thrown out of Disney World?"

"You know, they really didn't seem to."

"I'm glad you called, Lou—"

"I'm glad I called, too."

"I'm glad you called, because I was over at the house to-day—I thought maybe they'd sent my 1099 there—and I noticed that the radiator in the front hall was seeping. Did you bleed the radiators last fall?"

"Helena, I was thinking. Maybe we could all go to Europe this summer. I don't think the Soviet trip would be much fun for the kids, but I've got it down pretty well at this point. I can put someone else in charge for three or four weeks. We'll go to Poland, and Czechoslovakia, maybe even drive down to Bulgaria and take the kids to some monasteries. I think they're old enough to appreciate it. They really are good travelers, Helena. Very resourceful. Did Kitty tell you about the fountain?"

"Oh, Lou."

"Oh?"

"I can't take a month off. I'd lose all my shifts."

"Oh."

"It's a lovely idea, though. It really is. I think the kids would love it if you took them. We'll have to get them passports."

"Okay, Helena. It was just an idea. We'll see you in a couple of days."

"Tell Jonathan hi."

"I'll tell him."

Lou crossed the highway and looked out at the water, grey and opaque under a thin cloud cover. The seawall was under construction, and sections of concrete slab were stacked on the sand. He saw the boat launch a hundred yards up the beach, and two figures, knee-deep in the surf with their pant legs rolled up. It took him a minute to realize that he was looking at Jonathan and Kitty. They seemed so small.

The Endless Mountains

In 1976, the Bicentennial year, Jonathan turned twelve and started calling his father Lou. The two of them shared a room on the top floor of Lou's large brown-shingled Victorian in Cambridge, all the other bedrooms being occupied by paying tenants. Jonathan's younger sister, Kitty, lived in a nearby apartment with their mother. It was informal arrangement, though. Most summers Jonathan moved into the lower bunk in Kitty's room while Lou, who taught Slavic languages at Brandeis, was away leading camping tours of the Soviet Union. During the rest of the year he and Kitty made their way home together or separately after school as the mood suited them, sometimes wandering around until they got hungry and then fixing themselves a snack in whichever kitchen was closest.

One day at breakfast, Lou put down his newspaper and said he thought he'd walk to work.

"How far is it, Lou?" Jonathan asked.

"Ten miles, give or take."

"Can you really walk all the way?"

His father had never been athletic. His stomach hung over his belt. He smoked cigarettes and fed himself and Jonathan out of cans, which he bought in bulk from a wholesale grocer in Somerville.

"I'll just have to leave a little earlier," Lou said. "After all, Shulkin walked five thousand kilometers to escape the gulag." Shulkin was a colleague from Brandeis, a cheerful Russian man who wore overcoats and itchy-looking hats.

Lou got a ride home from school that day. He pulled

himself up the stairs, groaning, soaked in the tub for a long time, then went right to bed, leaving Jonathan to open a can of ravioli for supper. He persisted, though, walking to Brandeis again when he'd recovered from his first attempt, and after a few months he was jogging to work. His enthusiasms were always extreme. He checked nutrition books out of the library and began to make his own sprouts and yogurt, and a preparation he called "rejuvelac," which sat out on the pantry shelf in a water carafe. It had an eye-watering stench. He said it was the elixir of life and was disappointed when his kids refused to try it.

"It smells like diarrhea," Kitty said.

"Ah, but it merely tastes like vomit!"

At the Hippocrates Health Institute, he met some people who called themselves breatharians. "They live off the fruits and berries of the air," he told Jonathan. "Their bodies are so efficient that they subsist on sunlight and purified water. Can you imagine the lightness? There are documented cases of breatharians who have lived to be 130 years old."

Jonathan thought about his grandfather in Cleveland, who was 71. He had a hard time imagining Lou at Zadie's age, never mind 130.

"What would you do if you lived that long?" he asked.

"That's a problem I'd like to have."

On the first warm day of spring Lou bought himself and Jonathan ten-speed bicycles. They rode to Walden Pond and back, and up the industrial banks of the Merrimack River as far as Haverhill. They started talking about a big ambitious trip to Akron, Ohio, where Jonathan's aunt lived. Summer was out of the question—Lou would be gone, as usual. In any case, September was perfect biking weather, and he'd smooth it over with Jonathan's teacher. What of any real importance could Jonathan possibly miss in a week away from seventh grade?

All summer, in his lower bunk, Jonathan pored over a road atlas (feeling some gratification when Kitty complained about being left out). In his mind, the bike trip became a sort of audition for the Soviet Union: a chance to prove he was old enough and good enough company to take along next year. When Lou got home in late August they took a few shake-down rides, tuned their bikes, and went over their packing lists. In the interest of traveling light, Lou tore a bath towel in two and gave Jonathan half. They had to save room in their panniers for tools and maps, and a few discretionary items, like books and a deck of cards. A few days before setting off they convened in the living room, moving pushpins around a map on the wall.

"We can take the commuter line to Fitchburg," Lou said, sinking another pushpin. "That way we make Fisk's house the first night. He'll drive us to New Paltz in the morning."

"Why are we going to New Paltz?" Jonathan asked, suspicious.

"Fisk and I have to meet with Larson. But that should only take an hour or so."

Jonathan's father called his friends—most of them Slavicists like himself—by their last names, and this was how Jonathan knew them as well. For as long as he could remember, he and Kitty had called them Fisk and Larson and Grubsky and Stetz.

"Isn't it cheating, though?" he asked. "I thought we were going to ride our bikes the whole way."

Lou waved the objection off. "Don't be an ideologue," he said. "So we take a train. So we get a lift. The important thing is to travel by the seat of our pants. Anyhow, after New Paltz the real adventure begins. The Delaware River, the Alleghenies, *Scranton*. If we biked the whole way, we wouldn't have time to do Scranton properly."

Jonathan's legs felt rubbery as they pushed their bikes up Fisk's steep, rocky driveway. They'd ridden sixty miles—almost twice as far as they'd ever gone in one day. Fisk greeted them at the door of his cabin with a towel wrapped around his waist. "Schultz! Jonathan!" he said. "You made it! I've been heating up the sauna." His tiny cabin was dominated by a long wooden table, almost hidden under stacks of books, catalogues, loose papers, and dirty dishes. He'd set up two army cots in the small space between the table and his own bed, which was jammed up against a picture window. The shapes of several cars and trucks were visible in the darkening meadow out back.

In the sauna, Fisk—now without his towel—crouched on the slate floor feeding logs into the stove. His skin had turned pink, contrasting violently with his thick white hair and beard. Lou lay stretched out on the opposite bench, arms folded behind his head, sucking droplets of sweat out of his bushy moustache. The two men slipped in and out of Russian.

The heat made Jonathan woozy. "How long do we stay in here for?" he asked.

"How about we cool off in the river?" Fisk suggested.

They darted out into the chilly evening, across the driveway and down a mossy bank to the creek that ran through Fisk's property, yelping as they squatted in a deep part of the current. Fisk's beard glowed in the moonlight as he splashed himself with his long arms.

"Jonathan, one day I'll take you to the public baths in Leningrad," Lou said. "It's better than rejuvelac. You climb a ladder and sit on a shelf—the higher up you go, the hotter it is, until the steam is so thick you can't see your neighbor as he beats you with his *vennik*."

"What's a *vennik*?" Jonathan asked, his teeth chattering.

"A switch cut from a birch tree. Ah, you'd love it."

They ran up the bank and across the driveway, where

Jonathan and Lou had left their clothes in a pile outside the sauna, and dressed in the cabin.

"Officially, I've given up meat," Lou said as Fisk put a dish of beef stew in front of him, "but this smells too wonderful."

The men talked about Serbian verb stems until Jonathan's eyes began to droop. He put his bowl in the sink, spread out his sleeping bag, and opened his book, but he was asleep before he could find his place on the dog-eared page.

When Jonathan woke, his father was at the table arranging some wild mushrooms on a sheet of newspaper. "Hen of the Woods and some late chanterelles," he said. "We can have them for lunch. Larson will be delighted."

"We're staying there for lunch?"

"An early lunch. We'll hit the road right after and see if we can make it to the banks of the Delaware tonight."

Jonathan sat between his father and Fisk on the bench seat of Fisk's pickup truck, studying a New York State map while they talked across him. He counted just over fifty miles from New Paltz to the Delaware River. "When does it get dark, Lou?"

"Around seven o'clock, I'd say."

"How many miles an hour do you think we can go on our bikes?"

"For crying out loud, relax. I promise you, we'll be in Scranton by tomorrow afternoon."

Larson lived a few miles outside of New Paltz. His house was a gloomy little replica of Lou's, down to the cupola on the mossy roof. He hugged each of them for a long time before showing them into the living room. His wife, a Polish woman named

Olga, disappeared into the kitchen with Lou's mushrooms. Larson was one of Lou's oldest friends, but Jonathan could tell he annoyed Lou a little with his jowly, sad-eyed devotion. He wondered sometimes why his father was friends with Larson at all when he had so many other people to talk to about textbooks and verbs. Specifically, he wondered why they had to squander the morning here when Larson came to see them in Cambridge so often. Olga brought coffee for the men and a Fresca for Jonathan, and as he took the first swig, he realized he'd left his water bottle behind at Fisk's cabin.

While the Slavicists talked on, he thought about his water bottle. He pictured it sitting on the rough plank under Fisk's outdoor spigot. It was brand-new, white, with rings in the plastic that kept it snug in its bracket, and a thing on top that you pulled out so you could squirt water into your mouth without slowing down. He meant to say something, but Larson kept filling every conversational gap with appreciative murmurs and repetitions of Lou's comments. It wasn't until they'd loaded their panniers on their bikes and said goodbye to Fisk and the Larsons that he had a chance to mention it.

"Oh, Jonathan," Lou said. "Why didn't you speak up before Fisk drove away?"

They had to double back on Route 55 and find a bike shop in town. By the time they set off, it was after two. Lou hurried him up the long hill past Minnewaska State Park and down a busy stretch of Route 209.

Early the next afternoon they stood on a rise above Scranton looking down at a belt of factories surrounded by low hills. "An old coal town," Lou said. "Had its glory days around the turn of the century. Top-notch anthracite." The freight lines, spreading out across the valley, reminded Jonathan of one of his favorite stories: how Lou had hopped a train when he was fourteen — not much older than Jonathan was now. He'd gotten all the way to Enid, Oklahoma, and presented himself at the local jail, where they gave him a sandwich and a bed for the night. Jonathan must have seen something like it in a movie. In his mind's eye, the scene always ran in black and white.

They rode down into the valley, over tracks and under trestles, past warehouses and empty shopping centers, until the city streets began: storefronts, bus shelters, fire hydrants painted red white and blue for the Bicentennial.

"Hold up," Lou said, pulling over to the curb. "Look at that!" He pointed to a sign hanging over the entrance to a bar up the block. "*Zimne Piwo*. This must be a Polish neighborhood."

"What does *Zimne Piwo* mean?" asked Jonathan.

"Cold beer. *Zimne*: cold. *Piwo*: beer."

They went more slowly, looking around them.

Lou stopped again. What caught his attention was a red neon sign on the ground floor of a four-story brick building. "The Royal Czestochowa," it said. Through the window they saw long tables and hanging fluorescent light fixtures, and against the back wall, a cafeteria counter. The handwritten note taped to the double glass doors directed them to "enter throw hotel."

Two empty cement urns flanked the main entrance. Piped-in muzak followed them through a wide, high-ceilinged lobby lined with vinyl couches and into the dining room. A lady in a housecoat sat by the front window, motionless, a piece of toast suspended halfway between her plate and her open mouth.

"I'm famished," Lou said as they pushed their trays along the metal rail. He loaded up with a cucumber salad, a plate of pierogies, and three slices of black bread. "*Proszę, pan*," he called out to a man in a long apron who watched them from behind the cash register. "*Jest ten bigoş?*" He pointed at a vat of stew.

"*Tak, tak. Bigoş,*" the man said, shuffling over and picking up a ladle. He had the same moustache as Jonathan's father.

"You should try some of this," Lou said. "What the hell." He put a parfait glass of lime jello on his tray.

Jonathan accepted a bowl of bigoş. It smelled bad, like sauerkraut. He took some black bread, which he frosted with a thick layer of margarine, and inspected the jello. Suspended in it were pale, fuzzy pieces of canned fruit cocktail.

"This is where I'd like to spend my golden years," Lou said as they sat down with their trays. "Dozing in my oatmeal. Reading day-old newspapers. I could take a room upstairs."

Jonathan felt a momentary panic, as he always did when his father talked about retiring in some faraway place: Czechoslovakia, Sevastopol, Akron. He imagined for a second that he would be left behind, but then he remembered that Lou was talking about the future, when he would be older himself and living on his own.

The bigoş tasted even worse than it smelled. Jonathan chewed on a piece of bread and poked at his rubbery jello with a teaspoon. He considered whether he could get away with asking for a slice of pizza or a hot dog later, when they were exploring Scranton. The man in the apron was pushing a cart around the room now, tossing dishes into the bin and wiping the tables down with a rag. Lou said something to him in Polish, and soon the two of them were chatting away. Jonathan could see that it was not going to be easy to dislodge his father. He took a newspaper from the pile in the middle of the table. "School Bond Measure Passes"; "Wilkes-Barre Police Chief To Step Down"; and below the fold, "Mine Cave-in on Washburn St." The picture showed a house leaning at a strange angle, surrounded by traffic barriers.

He looked up Washburn Street on the map. "Lou," he said, "can we go see this?"

The house, when they found it, had tipped even farther back from the road. There was van with a gas company logo parked out front, but there was no sign of activity beyond the barricades. Yellow police tape was scattered in the front yard amid furniture, toys, soggy bedding, and trash bags with clothes spilling out of them.

"Ask not for whom the bell tolls, boychik," Lou said.

The windows of the house, tilted skyward, reflected steel-grey clouds gathering in the western sky.

In the morning they biked along the Lackawanna River, through Wilkes-Barre, then northwest on Highway 309. A few miles on, they hit the steepest climb of the trip so far. They switchbacked until traffic got too heavy, then inched up the breakdown lane. Jonathan's mind emptied of everything but forward motion. He strained against the pedals and stared at the small patch of road crawling beneath him, and when he looked up, he could no longer see his father. The grade steepened even more. Defeated, he got off his bike and walked, leaning his forearms on the handlebars. After a while he decided that pushing the bike was as much work as riding it, so he got back on, almost tipping over as he struggled to gain momentum on the hill. He found Lou resting under a tree in the next village with the map spread out in front of him. He leaned his bike against his father's and sat down heavily.

"Guess what they call this range we're in," Lou said.

Jonathan shrugged.

"The Endless Mountains."

When they set off again under thickening clouds, Jonathan was determined to get out front, or at least keep pace, but once again Lou pulled ahead. Every time Jonathan spotted him, the distance between them grew until his father disappeared entirely. The road went up and down along a ridge, neither losing nor gaining much altitude. Jonathan stared straight ahead, not looking at the countryside as it passed. He was glad to be alone now, relieved of the obligation to be good company. *"Eat my dust, Dad,"* he screamed through clenched teeth as he pushed up a hill, checking over his shoulder to be sure he was still alone.

Late in the afternoon, he spotted Lou's bike outside a trolley car diner and found him inside, sitting at the counter. A fry cook leaned on the counter in front of him, smoking. Seeing Jonathan, the cook stubbed out his cigarette and straightened up.

"Hey!" Lou said, swiveling around. "I was just talking about you. No one believes I have a twelve-year-old son who can ride his bike up a mountain."

"Mine don't do nothing but watch TV," the cook said. "Good for you, kid." He slapped the counter twice and turned back to the grill.

While they ate their sandwiches, Jonathan calculated their mileage on a napkin. He made a column of the distances between the little red arrows on the map, then added them up and checked his addition, going over their route to make sure he hadn't left anything out.

"Whattaya got?" Lou asked, mopping his plate with a bread crust.

"Fifty-seven miles so far."

"Let me see the map." He put on his reading glasses. "How are you holding up?"

"Good."

"Why don't we bypass Williamsport, then? Let's see if we can make it here." He pointed at a town where the road they were following intersected Route 15.

When the rain came, it wasn't a soaking one. It softened the line of trees and released perfume from the yellowing ferns alongside the road. Jonathan passed a sign that said, "State Game Lands Number 134." He realized he hadn't seen a house for miles. At Route 15 he found Lou waiting outside a boarded-up gas station.

"It looks like the town's gone," Lou said.

"You said there would be a motel."

"I guess I was wrong."

The mountain air atomized their breath. "I'm cold," Jonathan said."

"I don't know what to tell you," Lou said. "We can turn around and go to Williamsport if that's what you want."

"No, I don't want to backtrack."

"Good. Neither do I."

They pushed on, riding together now. They put on their headlamps when it got dark. Trees, fields, collapsing sheds, clusters of trailers scrolled past in the thin bands of light until they came to a darkened house. The residents had turned in for the night or moved away; they couldn't tell which, and they decided not to knock on the door. Exhausted, they spread out their sleeping bags on the wide front porch and ate a dinner of sardines and crackers. Lou rolled up his half-towel for neck support—a habit he'd picked up in Japan when he was in the army—and Jonathan wadded his pants and shirt into a pillow.

A freight train blasted by in the middle of the night, so close it shook the porch, and for a moment Jonathan didn't know where he was. Then he saw his panniers and his sneakers, stuffed with newspaper to soak up the day's rain. The sky was clear now. The moon, high over the trees across the road, flooded the porch with light. He could count every link on the chain of his bicycle, leaning against the rail in front of him.

"Lou, are you awake?"

"Hmm."

"Lou?"

"Hmm?"

"Did your dad ever go with you?"

"Go where?"

"You know, like the time you went to Oklahoma?"

"No," Lou said, "Zadie had to mind the store." He adjusted his towel. "We've got a big climb tomorrow, Jonathan." Soon he was snoring softly, inhaling and exhaling the fruits and berries of the air.

While Jonathan waited for sleep to return, he thought of Lou at fourteen—just a few years older than he was now—running alongside a slow-moving train, grabbing on to the side. Lou had stopped snoring. When Jonathan looked over he was lying perfectly still, washed in a cold light. Jonathan went back to his reverie.

A dark, flat place sped past the open door of the boxcar. It was all he could summon when he thought of Oklahoma. The train slowed, then stopped in a sleeping town. This time, though, instead of his father, Jonathan saw himself turning his pockets inside out for the man at the jail.

Moscow, 1968

Helena's three-family building sat on the back half of a divided lot on the Cambridge–Somerville line, tucked in behind another house. A trellis, sagging from the weight of a Concord grape vine, covered the flagstone walk. Crushed fruit littered the concrete steps leading to the porch, where all the names on the mailboxes gave an impression of serious overcrowding. Below Helena's name on the third floor mailbox was that of her son, Jonathan. He lived in Jamaica Plain but registered his car in Cambridge. A long list of Tanzanian names covered the second floor mailbox: Membe, Batenga, Bukurura, Amani, etc. There were actually only three single men living in the apartment, but not always the same three. As they moved in and out, the list was appended with new names, written on masking tape in various hands. On the mailbox for the first floor, along with "Gulnaev"—Helena's Section 8 tenants, a family from Chechnya—were several other Chechen surnames; probably relatives using their address for some official business.

It had been a nice little junkyard district when Helena bought the building fifteen years earlier, in the early '90s—only a few houses on her end of the block. Since then, condominium complexes and parking garages had sprung up everywhere. Her building was hemmed in on three sides, but her south windows faced the open sky above her neighbor's back yard. One moonlit night, Helena and Jonathan had sneaked past the neighbor's house with two passive solar panels and installed them on south wall of her building to supplement the forced-air heating system. The results had been disappointing, though, and now she was blowing insulation into the ceiling of her kitchen with a machine she'd rented by the hour. She worked slowly. At seventy-one, she'd become unsteady on a stepladder. Insulation escaped from the keyholes she'd cut in the drywall before she had a chance to cover them up, and clouds of itchy fluff blew around the room, sticking to her sweaty arms and neck and to her tights. The hose kept clogging. Each time, she had to climb down, turn off the machine, and pull the impacted wad out of the nozzle. She was beginning to worry that she wouldn't make it back to the rental place before they closed.

She heard a knock on the back door and descended the ladder carefully. Zabet, one of the Chechens from the first floor, stood in the dark stairwell holding a Pyrex dish. Zabet's hair, cut stylishly short and dyed a reddish brown when Helena had last seen it, was covered now with a black hijab. It made a striking combination with her thin, gracefully arched eyebrows, which were tattooed on—as were her eye- and lip-liner. Helena smoothed the fluffs of insulation from her own hair and asked Zabet in. The Gulnaevs were political refugees. They had been living in Helena's first-floor apartment for seven and a half years. Zabet and her husband, Axmet, had two children: a son, Adlan, now twenty, and his sister Alla, who was seventeen and no longer living at home. All of them were dark and lithe, with long, straight noses and intelligent, almond-shaped eyes. Their beauty somehow made their problems seem more tragic.

When they first arrived, Zabet often came to Helena for help. Helena welcomed the opportunity to use her college Russian. She read employment ads for Zabet and helped her apply for food stamps. These were the sorts of things she'd dealt with herself thirty-five years earlier when she was newly divorced, with a son and a daughter of her own. She found charter schools for the children. Also a Balkan choir, a homework club, and a dance school that offered sliding scale tuition.

At first Helena had a hard time making sense of their story—because her Russian was rusty, and because they'd moved around so much. Axmet and Zabet had met as college students in Novosibirsk and fallen in love, to the disappointment of both families, who'd had other plans for them. They'd lived in Grozny and in Zabet's home country of Dagestan before settling in Kyrgyzstan, where Axmet had relatives. Then, around the time of the second Chechen war, Axmet had lost his job. Zabet described arrests and beatings—sometimes attributing them to ethnic hatred, sometimes to bad luck or random chance, sometimes to professional or family jealousies. Even when Helena didn't understand the words—*visilat*, *obvinyat*—she could guess their meanings from Zabet's dramatic expressions.

During the their few years in Cambridge, things seemed to go all right for the Gulnaevs. Helena helped Zabet pay for a cosmetics course, and she got a job in a salon in Brookline, where the clients were mostly Russian Jews. Axmet found work at a muffler shop. Somehow, though, setbacks always outpaced advances, and they weren't quite able to cover their expenses. Axmet had health problems. Adlan graduated from high school and enrolled in classes at Bunker Hill Community College, but he dropped out within a few months. Zabet told Helena it was because his classes were too easy—that he was planning to apply to some real colleges.

As their problems mounted, the family seemed to retrench. Zabet and Alla began covering their hair. Adlan grew a beard and began attending a local mosque. Only Axmet was unaltered; he still shaved and wore work pants, running shoes, and fitted t-shirts that showed off his boxer's physique. Then, unexpectedly, they took Alla out of school. The concern was that she was "having boyfriends."

"She's becoming a wild girl, Galina," Zabet explained. "You don't know how wild."

While Helena was still thinking of a way to get Alla back in school, she learned of her engagement to a Chechen boy whose uncle was a wealthy businessman in Kazakhstan.

"Does she want this?" Helena asked.

"Yes," Zabet said. "She wants *away*."

Alla and her new husband would live in Almaty. She could finish school there, Zabet said. She was interested in the law, or maybe social work. Helena couldn't honestly say her prospects there were worse in Almaty than in Cambridge. Somehow, though, she ended up back in Chechnya living with her in-laws. In Grozny, of all places, where the Gulnaevs' journey had begun. Within a year she had a baby.

Zabet handed Helena the Pyrex dish and stepped into the kitchen. "I brought you cabbage with meats and rice. I think you like this before."

"*Golubtsy*," insisted Helena. "*Bolshoi spasiba*."

"Yes, of course, *golubtsy*." She collapsed in a chair. "Oh, Galina!" This was what she called Helena. "Is problem with Alla. She is in Grozny hospital."

Helena sat down across the table and winced. "Alla is sick?"

"She have a fever, very high fever, and pain in stomach."

"What do the doctors say?"

"Well, you know Movladi's mother make her work too hard."

Helena had heard this already. It was much as Zabet would reveal of any misgivings. "But do they know why she has a fever? Is it some kind of infection?"

"Yes, infection."

"What kind of infection? What's wrong with her?"

Zabet tugged nervously on the sleeve of her sweater. "I wish she could go to Kizlyar. To the better hospital, for antibiotics." Zabet's family was in Kizlyar, just over the Dagestan border.

Helena shook her head, not understanding. "They aren't treating her? No antibiotics?"

"Of course, but I call this morning and she still have a high fever. I don't think they are giving her real drugs. You have to pay to make sure they give her real drugs, not counterfeit. I know the doctor in Kizlyar to get them."

"Maybe she should come back here if she's sick."

"No, no—is better there."

Helena didn't have the heart to mount a defense of the American medical system. She submitted to it herself only when starkly necessary.

"How much money do you think you'll need for this?"

"Well, something else. I wish I could go to Kizlyar, to take care from her. And I know we already owe you. I have some necklace that I can sell. Antique necklace. I can show you. But I'm asking, can you lend the money now?"

Zabet's face, a pale oval inscribed by black fabric, was pinched with fear for Alla. Of course Helena would give her the money, but she already felt the drag of futility.

It was 8:30. She'd have to keep the insulation blower for another day.

Axmet leaned into the engine of Jonathan's Subaru, listening. Jonathan liked Axmet very much. He was compact and muscled, and Jonathan particularly admired his shapely Caucasian moustache. He could be moody, sometimes passing Jonathan in the stairwell of his mother's building without a greeting, but there was usually a kind of conspiratorial manliness about their interactions that Jonathan found flattering. A few times he had even been invited into the Gulnaevs' kitchen for a glass of brandy, which had been served in a cordial glass from a mirror-lined credenza jammed up against the fridge.

"Bad sparkplug wires," Axmet said, straightening up.

"Didn't you change them last month when you tuned it?"

Axmet shrugged cryptically and closed the hood. He had been a mechanical engineer back in Chechnya, but Jonathan suspected that he was not a very good auto mechanic. His repairs were never without complications. For instance, the Subaru had been guzzling fuel since the tune-up. Jonathan was loath to complain, though, because Axmet had only charged him for parts (air filter, points, plugs, and *wires*). Axmet himself had insisted on listening to the engine just now; he'd been sitting on a kitchen chair on the sidewalk when Jonathan pulled up.

"I can replace wires."

"Well, I'm kind of running around today, Axmet."

"Leave the key, Jonathan! I can fix it now."

"I told my mother I'd take her to Home Depot. Can I look for you in an hour or so?"

"Of course, Jonathan!"

This was all part of a complex system of barter between his mother and the Gulnaevs. Axmet worked on his Subaru and Helena's Civic. She'd had eyeliner tattooed on her face at Zabet's salon. (The idea creeped Jonathan out). Zabet was always bringing food upstairs: black bread or borscht or some Chechen dish. All this was in exchange for rent forgiven—their mandated contribution to the Section 8 payment. And, he suspected, other favors. As much as he liked Axmet, Jonathan found the Gulnaevs frustrating and depressing. The stories his mother told him about them were full of baroque Chechen problems requiring Chechen solutions: bribes, arranged marriages,

Soviet-era medicine. It seemed to him that the family was not any better off after seven years of his mother's interventions, and he wondered if she would have become so involved with them if they were from somewhere else. On her bookshelf: Ouspensky, Gurdjieff, Idries Shah.

"Tell your mother dryer is fixed," Axmet called out as Jonathan climbed the front steps. "Tell her it was thermal fuse. And thanks her again. For Alla."

Jonathan found Helena in her kitchen. She poured her coffee into a mayonnaise jar, screwed on the lid, and put the jar in her purse—one of her bizarre habits of thrift.

"Axmet says to thank you for Alla. What does that mean, thanks for Alla?"

By the set of his mother's jaw, he could tell she'd loaned them more money.

"What do you need at Home Depot?" he asked when she didn't answer his first question.

"A door." She belted her jacket. "For the dining room in the first floor. Zabet is bringing Alla back from Dagestan in a few days with her baby, and they need turn it back into a bedroom."

"Alla's moving back in?"

"Zabet doesn't want to leave her with her husband's family while she's recuperating."

"Recuperating from what?"

Helena waited until they were in Jonathan's car to answer. "The doctors said it was herpes simplex five."

"Simplex *five*? I've never heard of that. Did her husband pick it up from a hooker?"

She frowned. "I should do some childproofing."

"How long is she staying?"

"I don't know. I'm hoping she doesn't go back at all. Zabet didn't come out and say it, but I think her husband has been abusing her."

"Jesus. What next?"

Helena looked tired under the fluorescent lights at Home Depot. As she reached up for a package of cabinet latches, Jonathan noticed that her tights had worn through at the heels. It infuriated him to think how the Gulnaevs must see his mother: a rich American landlady. "You should get the cheapest piece of hollow-core shit they have, Mom," he said as they walked through the aisle of doors, craning their necks.

"Hah. You sound like Adlan. I asked him what happened to the old door, and he said he threw it away. 'I never saw a piece of shit like that before I moved to your country.' That's what he said." She leafed through the doors on the rack like pages in a newspaper. "The cheapest six-panel is eighty dollars, without the hardware. Maybe I can get something at the salvage yard."

The rest of them were depressing. Adlan, though, Jonathan actively disliked. He assumed Adlan, who struck him as some kind of charlatan with his skull cap and hiphop pants, was behind the family's religious turn—and therefore, he assumed, this latest misery.

"Why do you let him talk to you like that?" he said. "They aren't even paying rent."

"Yes they are."

"You told me they weren't."

"I'm getting Section 8," she said crossly.

"I know that. But you said they were supposed to be paying some of it themselves."

"Axmet lost his job. Zabet's hours got cut back."

"Of course they cut her hours back. Who wants to get make-up tattooed on their face by a lady in a burka?"

"It's not a burka. It's a hijab."

"Anyhow, I guarantee you Section 8 did not approve that apartment for four adults and a baby."

Helena took the mayonnaise jar out of her pocketbook and unscrewed the lid. "Maybe it *would* be better if Alla and her baby stayed upstairs with me."

"What? Where are they going to sleep?" Helena had two bedrooms in her apartment, but one was stripped down to the studs and completely filled with tools. "*Mom?*"

"I heard you. They can sleep in my room, of course." She screwed the lid back on without taking a drink.

"And where are *you* going to sleep?"

"The sofa pulls out."

Jonathan enjoyed telling people about his mother's crazy building: the Chechens, the Tanzanians, sneaking around with the passive solar panels. Still, the thought of her in her flannel nightgown, stacking the cushions on the floor and pulling out the sofa bed, of the dusty old blankets he remembered from his own childhood, her scratched reading glasses and pill bottles on the cluttered end table—the whole picture filled him with shame.

Helena had spent a week removing the old shingles from the front wall of her building—a job that should not have taken more than a few days. She pulled out the nails with a cat's paw, bundled them with twine, and stacked them in the alley on the side of the house so she could put them out for the trash men a few bundles at a time. Now she was nailing on new shingles, working from the ground up. She used a chalk line to keep the courses straight. She was almost up to the second floor windows. Looking around, she saw that she'd forgotten to bring the level with her the last time she moved the plank.

Axmet sat on a kitchen chair at the end of the flagstone walk, looking out at the street. It had become his regular spot in the last few months. Helena called out to him: "Axmet, can you pass me that level?" He didn't turn around, so she called again, louder this time, and he jumped up. "I'm sorry. I didn't mean to startle you. Could you pass me the level?"

He got up and steadied himself against the neighbor's house.

"Are you okay?" she asked.

"Headache."

Helena knelt on the plank and reached down as far as she could. He passed the level into her extended hand. "Thank you," she said. "I'm so tired of climbing up and down. So, Axmet, did Alla tell you about the place we looked at?"

"What place?"

"Horizon House." She held the level up to the course of shingles and used her cat's paw to pry loose the one she'd just nailed on. "They offer GED classes. Alla shouldn't need much help, though; she could probably pass the test if she took it today. But they do have some job training."

"Alla is going to college?" Axmet looked confused.

"No. Well, maybe. It's more like a residential program."

"Why Alla don't stay here?"

"I'm not sure it's . . . well, do you think it's safe for Alla and her baby to stay here right now?"

"Why not is safe?"

"You know her husband's been calling, right? Threatening to send someone to take the baby?"

His face hardened. "Don't worry Movladi. I can take care Movladi." He sat back down on his chair, facing away from the house.

Upstairs in her apartment, Helena found Zabet sitting on the sofa with Alla's baby, a curly-haired little girl named Malina.

"Galina, come sit!" Zabet moved the baby onto her lap and

patted the cushion next to her.

"Just give me a moment," Helena said, taking off her tool belt.

"I am showing Malina her mother's wedding video. Sit for a minute."

Helena sat down.

A snow-topped mountain, a sky of impossible blue. A waterfall dissolving into a beautiful sunset. A pure white dove gliding across the screen, peeling away the sunset with its beak to reveal the image beneath: three old women chopping vegetables in an outdoor kitchen. "Those are Movladi's aunties," Zabet said. She pressed fast-forward as a wedding tent went up in juddering video frames. She took her thumb off the button to show Adlan offering a stack of dollar bills to another young man. "Movladi. This is, they are pretending only. A—"

"A ritual?" asked Helena."

"Yes, a ritual. See, Movladi turn him away."

Young women danced across a cement courtyard in long, brightly colored dresses, hands held high in elegant shapes. Zabet's free hand twisted with the rhythm of the pandur music in the background. "See, Malinochka? Your mother is the best dancer. You remember, Galina. You take her to dance class."

More chopping of vegetables. Cartoon animals scampered through the scene—a squirrel, a deer, a porcupine.

"Movladi's family pay a lot of money for this video," Zabet said. "Is the best director in Almaty."

Now the camera followed a line of white Mercedes limousines, and now a row of men in dark, old-fashioned clothes sitting on wooden chairs. Helena recognized Axmet among them. She was startled for a moment, as though she had spotted him in a Stalin-era ethnographic film.

"Zabet, how is Axmet doing? He didn't seem well when I saw him just now."

Zabet sucked air between her teeth: *tsstch*. "You know his headache get all the time worse. And he don't eat without throwing up."

"What does the doctor say?"

"The doctor said he have to stop working, he need resting. But what working?" She offered a palm to the sky.

The camera wobbled around a room full of women, stopping at Alla in her wedding dress. Zabet was fixing the veil on her head, which was surrounded by yellow cartoon birds.

"There," Zabet said, hitting pause. "There, see?" Handing the baby to Helena, she got up and tapped the screen. "One of my necklace—garnet and pearl. That one is Alla's favorite. Galina, I have to get dinner started. There's a bottle in the fridge for Malina, and Alla will coming home soon. She say 5:30, latest." She kissed Malina on the cheek and let herself out the back door.

Helena carried Malina to the kitchen and put her in her high chair. The baby reached up expectantly with her starfish hand, and Helena gave her a spoon—something for her to bang on her tray.

"Buh," said Malina.

"Buh," answered Helena.

"Buh BAH."

Helena was thinking about Alla's wedding dress, its scoop neck and princess sleeves. She wondered if Alla wore her head-scarf and abaya in Grozny.

The front door slammed, then the bedroom door. Helena picked up the baby. She found Alla in the bedroom, dumping her suitcases out on the floor. The recent illness had made her face narrower, and Helena was struck by how different she looked from the girl in the video. She pushed her sleeves back and clawed through the pile. She still had on the thin black rubber bracelets she'd worn in high school—a dozen on each wrist.

"What are you looking for?" Helena asked.

"Malina's passport." She extracted it from a zippered pouch and tried to tear it in half, then started ripping out pages and crumpling them.

"Stop that, Alla, and tell me what happened."

Alla dropped the passport and leaned against the bed. "He says I have to send her to Movladi's family." She spoke loudly to even out the tremor in her voice. Her eyes watered, and she bent forward, hiding her face.

"Who said that?"

"Papa," she said through her hands. "I can't believe you told him about Horizon House."

"Oh, Alla, I'm so sorry. I didn't know it was a secret."

"Did you tell him about the herpes, too?"

"Of course not!" But she wasn't sure. Had she mentioned it?

Malina whined and twisted toward her mother. Helena set her down on the floor next to Alla. "I'm sorry," she said again, and she really was. Nothing she did turned out right.

Jonathan's mother looked up at him anxiously while he disassembled the top layer of scaffolding. He could see it was killing her not to be holding the hammer herself.

"I would have come over and helped you with the shingles if you'd said something."

"I didn't *need* help with the shingles. I just need you to loosen those couplings for me."

She was wearing a wraparound skirt and a sleeveless blouse. Her legs were covered in bruises. He noticed that her hair, pinned in a messy bun on top of her head, had turned from blonde to white.

"You can't do this by yourself," he said. He hammered in

silence for a while. "You know—" He stopped himself.

"What? What do I know?"

He turned around. "Okay. You could hire someone to do this shit for you if you'd stop giving your money away."

"I don't want to hire someone." Her mouth was puckered stubbornly. "I'm perfectly capable of shingling my own house. And it was a loan."

Jonathan exhaled "Right, the necklaces. I forgot." He went back to hammering. "They aren't your family," he said. "You *have* a family. If they were your family, Adlan would be up here doing this instead of strutting around like a holy pimp. Treating his own sister like chattel."

"You don't know anything about it," Helena said, shouting over the clang of Jonathan's hammer.

"I know you think you're helping, but you're not," he said reasonably. "Throwing money at those people will not solve their problems."

When he looked down again, she'd gone inside the house. He'd resolved to go upstairs and make some sort of conciliatory gesture when she reappeared, holding a sheet of paper.

"Axmet asked me to show you this," she said. "Adlan's college essay. He wants a *man's* opinion." She handed it up to him and went back inside.

> *I would like to thank the Admission Committee for wondering to know more about me. As you will see in my record, I am a very good student in math, and also Physics. I hope to be a mechanical engineer one day, so it is not important that I don't have such a good marks in English and some other subjects, though of course I love the English Language very much. Also, that I graduated from Highschool over two years ago.*
>
> *One more thing you might like to know about me is*

the person I most admire. This Person is my father, Mr.
Axmet Gulnaev, age 45. He is a strong Patriarch of our
family, when we came seven years ago from Chechnya.
In Chechnya, as you may know, we have two wars so
that we can be a free country from Russia. This is what
I admire most about America that it became free from
Britain after much bloodshed and courage and it is no
different for Chechnya. I admire Axmet Gulnaev be-
cause he was kidnaped by the police and beaten, but he
took us his family, to this country. My father was is was
a mechanical engineer in Chechnya, as I will be one
here. That is the other think I admire about America,
that anyone who works hard will get his reward.

In the jewelry stores up and down Newbury Street, they'd tak-
en one look at Zabet's hijab and directed her elsewhere, hands
hovering above panic buttons. That was what she told Helena.

"You think I was carrying bomb," she said.

Someone told her about a specialist in Downtown Crossing who bought antique jewelry for private clients. They knew
what she had, but they didn't think she did.

"'Where did you get this?' They ask me that, and then they
insulted me with their offers."

She took the necklaces to Brookline, where she hoped her
Russian would do her some good, but no one offered even a
quarter of what they were worth. Finally, an appraiser told her
that the market for her jewelry was in Moscow, so the Gulnaevs
pooled their money and bought her a plane ticket. She had an
appointment that Axmet's cousin's husband's college roommate set up.

"I'd love to see Moscow again," Helena said to Zabet on
the way to the airport.

"You have been to Moscow, Galina?"

"I was there in, let's see, 1968. With my first husband."

"1968," Zabet said wonderingly. "That was a long time ago." She opened her pocketbook and checked to see that she had remembered all her documents. "Thank you for looking after Alla and Malina," she added in Russian.

"*Ne problema.* No problem."

"Oh," she said, returning to English, "This is insurance card for Axmet. I don't let him keep it, because he will lose. Can you remind him he have doctor appointment on Friday?"

"Friday. Yes, what time?"

"Friday at ten."

"I'll make sure he gets there," Helena said. "I'll take care of everything."

She stopped at the curb outside the international terminal. She meant to wait until Zabet got inside, but a shuttle van pulled up behind her and honked. As soon as she got home, exhaustion overtook her and she lay down on the sofa. The shingling was done and she'd replaced two windows, but she'd meant to accomplish so much more, and now the summer was over.

She closed her eyes and saw Moscow, washed in Instamatic green.

Monumental plazas, fountains lined with tulips. Streets nearly empty; shop windows displaying Bulgarian canned goods in sparse pyramids. Zabet steps off a green and white electric tram. Her hair is cut stylishly short and dyed a reddish brown. She looks at the street name high up on the corner building. She shows a piece of paper to an old grandmother sweeping the sidewalk in front of a store, and follows her indicating gesture through a gate to an inner courtyard.

Zabet comes out of her appointment smiling. The envelope she's holding bulges with hard currency. She crosses to the median island of the wide boulevard, disappears briefly behind a passing bus, and reappears on the opposite sidewalk in front of a kiosk, the kind that sells sausages and piroshki and potatoes stuffed with herring. She changes her mind, and instead, she walks a few blocks west and crosses the Borodinsky Bridge to the market near the Kievsky train station. She'll buy some bread and apricots, and maybe some tomatoes, the kind they grow in Kizlyar: deep red, almost the color of plums. She'll eat her picnic on a bench in the vaulted waiting room of the station. Zabet is gone.

The Cloud of Unknowing

Meanwhile the Corinthians completed their prepara-
tions and sailed for Corcyra with a hundred and fifty
ships. Of these Elis furnished ten, Megara twelve, Leu-
cas ten, Ambracia twenty-seven—

Kitty's eyes slid off the page and up to the bleary halo of
light surrounding the lamppost outside the library window.
She was a slow reader. The syllabus for Humanities 110—
Herodotus, Hesiod, Thucydides, mandatory for all Reed College freshmen—had defeated her last semester, and she'd taken
an incomplete. Then, instead of reading *The Peloponnesian
War*, she'd spent her break in a stupor watching Jack Benny
reruns as 1982 wound down. It was February now, cold and
green, and the bare branches of the cherry trees along the campus paths were dark in the Portland drizzle. In another month
they would be swelling with buds.

Each of these contingents had its own admiral, the Cor-
inthians being under the command of Xenoclides, son
of Euthycles—

Her eyes slid again. The steam heat was making her drowsy.
She resolved to finish the chapter at home.

Outside the library, she stood for a moment looking back
at the vaulted windows of the reserve room. It was a beautiful
building: turrets and ivy and gothic arches, everything she'd
imagined when she'd fantasized about going away to college,

but she was glad to turn from it now. She cut across the lawn, soaking her tennis shoes instantly. The air was saturated with something between a heavy mist and a light rain. A searchlight raked the low sky somewhere beyond the river, miles away. She walked in that direction, following the slope of Woodstock Boulevard.

It wasn't until Kitty left campus that it became real—the distance between Oregon and the New England city where she'd grown up. The streets to the south of Woodstock were wide, curving arbitrarily past low houses landscaped with strange conifers and succulents and gravel that glowed like moon rock under tall western streetlights. Up the hill from campus the houses were bigger and older, but not like the big old houses back home. They lacked ornamentation. The roofs of their wide porches were supported by a kind of column she didn't remember seeing before: square and tapering, like a crude optical illusion. In her mind, those houses were closer to lumber than the shingled and gabled Victorians in her town. They made her think of the great trees that stood in every direction outside the city.

Kitty had lived up the hill from campus for a few months. Midway through the fall semester she'd moved out of her dormitory and into a group house with some older students. She'd been infatuated with someone who lived there, but things had ended badly with him. She moved again, right before the fall break, into another big house—this one on a cul-de-sac off Powell Boulevard, a mile and a half north of campus: her third address in six months, each a little farther afield.

She crossed 28th Street at the bottom of the hill. From the 7-Eleven parking lot, she could read the big clock inside the store. It was only 11:40. Now she wished she'd stayed at the library until closing. She had a question for Jim, but he worked the graveyard shift. He wouldn't be there for another twenty minutes, and she didn't want him to find her waiting. "Don't come too often," he had said the first time she visited him at work. She hadn't been offended, though. She'd accepted it as a kind of intimacy.

She walked home along 28th Street past small, temporary-looking houses, and apartment complexes that reminded her of motels, with their rows of parking spots and numbered doors. Turning onto Powell, she left the residential streets behind. Two cars idled side-by-side outside the all-night bowling alley across the highway. She stood for a moment admiring the reflection of their taillights on the wet pavement. On rare sunny days she could see the snowcap of Mount Hood rising above the boulevard, but on a rainy night it could be anywhere.

Kitty's street dead-ended at the locked gate of a fuel company. Hers was the only house on the block, next to the drive-thru window of a Wendy's that fronted on Powell. Sometimes she sat on the back porch and listened to the voices on the speaker box. *Good afternoon, sir. Would you like to try our new baked stuffed potato? It comes in four exciting flavors. We have chili, sour cream and chive, cheddar cheese and chive, and ranch* — over and over, until the flare and crackle of the speaker was a little like surf hitting sand. She got to know the voices of the different girls who worked there. When she had no classes and could stay home all day, she would go next door and buy a small coffee and sweeten it to syrup. She'd stuff some crackers and hot sauce in her pockets for lunch, and return for coffee refills until her cup was too soggy to use.

She shared the house with three other Reedies, but she had her own entrance: a side door opening into the basement. Her room was partitioned off by a plywood wall. It had been built as a practice space for a band whose members had lived in the house at some point. They'd cut Styrofoam inserts to fit into the narrow windowsills. She pulled them out, but she could do nothing about the spray-on soundproofing that hung like dust from the ceiling. The lighting, too, was ghastly: a double fluorescent fixture. One tube was strobing. She kept meaning to look for a replacement in the basement clutter outside her room.

She hung her coat on the pipe running along the ceiling, took off her wet tennis shoes, and went upstairs. A light-gray cat was on the kitchen counter, licking at a stick of butter.

"Come on, Windex. We can do better than that," she said, shaking some dry food into the cat's bowl. She'd found the little cat on the back porch a few weeks earlier and taken her into the house, and so far, none of her roommates had said anything. It was possible they hadn't noticed. They weren't around much. The name, Windex, was her private joke, an answer to the campus dogs that lounged on the floor of the Student Union: Wittgenstein, Antigone, Mingus. Windex purred while she ate, and Kitty put a saucepan of water on the stove for oatmeal. It was all she had in the house besides cat chow. She dressed it with some extra cream and sugar packets she'd stolen from Wendy's and carried it downstairs, Windex close at her heels.

She sat at her writing desk and pulled the books out of her backpack. She opened *The Peloponnesian War*, then put it down again and picked up *Dionysius the Areopagite* instead. She'd taken an incomplete in that course too—Western Mystical Philosophy. She still had to write the term paper. The reading was denser, but there was a lot less of it. Lately she'd found that she could become immersed if she read closely and tried to follow the arguments. Maybe it was the effect of her new room: monkish and cell-like. There was a thrill of secret initiation that, had she been raised in a religion, she would have recognized.

She took an index card out of her desk and copied out a passage. "For if all the branches of knowledge belong to things that have being, then that which is beyond Being must also be transcendent above all Knowledge." She read it over and added, "Cf Cloud of Unknowing." She'd made a pile of notes already, but she didn't know what to do with the ideas as a group. That was what she'd wanted to talk to Jim about tonight. He'd mentioned something to her the last time she'd talked to him, some theory that God is a sentence without meaning, or maybe a grammatical formula for making all the sentences of the world.

The first time Kitty saw Jim was on a sunny September afternoon just a few weeks after she'd arrived on campus. She was still enjoying a kind of automatic popularity with some of the older guys. She sat on the steps of the student union with someone she'd just met, a Chemistry major from New York City named Conrad. He was telling her about Renaissance Fair, a campus-wide "bacchanal" that marked the end of the school year in May. He used the word as though it were a neutral term, like "prom" or "social." She was only half-listening, though. While he talked, her eyes followed someone walking across the lawn. He wore a red and black checked hunting cap and work pants and a matching jacket, like a TV repairman's uniform. He took long steps, swinging his arms almost comically. From where they sat, a hundred feet away, Kitty sensed a coiled energy.

Conrad noticed her looking. "That's Jim Frank," he said. "He's a real wild man. Do you want to meet him? *Hey Jim,*" he called, "do you want to meet my friend Kitty?" Kitty got the impression he was showing off a little, pleased with himself for knowing this person well enough to make an introduction. The walker stopped and pivoted in their direction. "*No!*" he called back, flashing a wide grin. He continued on the path, disappearing into the campus radio station—which was in the basement of Kitty's dorm block.

Half an hour later Kitty was sitting on the toilet in a bathroom stall on her dormitory floor when Jim Frank's face appeared between the door and the frame.

"Pleased to meet you, Kitty," he said. He stuck his hand through the gap. His gray, unblinking eyes met hers directly, and she stared back until her pee stream stopped.

"I'll be right out," she said.

She found him in the hallway, bouncing lightly in his black service oxfords. "I apologize," he said. "About before, I mean. I don't like that guy. I didn't want to talk to him."

"Conrad said you were a wild man."

He nodded vigorously. "That's it, right there. That's why I don't like him."

They went outside and fell naturally to walking. Jim clasped his hands behind his back. Kitty sensed that he was concentrating on matching her pace; that he would be walking faster if he were by himself. He was from the Bay Area. He'd dropped out a year earlier and he wasn't sure if he was going to stay in Portland. He told Kitty he was writing a novel, and that he found inspiration in California: the tiki torches at night, the smell of barbecue.

"Listen, Kitty," he said, "can you do me a favor? I need something from the library. *The Thief's Journal*, Jean Genet. I don't have an ID anymore. I was going to ask my friend who works at the radio station, but he wasn't around."

"I mean, I'd like to help, but—"

"I'll give you my driver's license as collateral. I only need it for a day."

She brought the book out to him and he handed her his driver's license. He had a beard in the picture.

Kitty took Jim's license out and looked at it a few times that evening. When he met her on the library steps the next day to give her the book, he didn't want it back. "It's expired anyhow," he said. And that was the last she saw of Jim for several months.

Kitty saw Conrad all the time. He always seemed to be hanging around the Student Union or the coffee shop next door. She liked his rapid way of speaking and his Converse high tops and his hair—long and kinky and black, like Jimmy Page. They hung out together all night at the first social of the year. Kitty was wearing an old dress of her mother's—burgundy rayon with a square neckline and short, puffed sleeves that made her look like a cigarette girl. They danced until their clothes clung to them, and then Conrad leaned in to be heard over the band, enclosing her in a curtain of kinky hair. "Let's go to the rhodo garden," he said. His lips brushed her ear.

What? She asked with her eyes.

"The rhododendron garden. Down the hill. I'll show you."

She followed him down the steep campus driveway, across 28th Street, and into the quiet park. The path wound among bushes and over a little footbridge. *Something is about to happen now*, she thought as they sat down on the bank of the pond. She felt a pulsing in her throat and between her legs. Without hesitating, Conrad kissed her, forcing her down onto the grass. Thinking of duck shit, she pushed him away and pulled off her mother's rayon dress. He stood up and straddled her while he undressed, then knelt down and wriggled her underwear off. His face loomed close again, and then he was lying on her. She wrapped her legs around him and memorized the patch of sky over his shoulder, and the rhododendron branches framing it.

And then he was inside her and she was moving with him, her arms pinned on the spongy ground. All of him felt smooth and hard. She smelled his hair. *Prell*, she thought. He jerked forward suddenly and gasped, and then they were lying side by side. He slid his hand over her shoulder, down into the dip of her waist, and up over her hip. She still throbbed everywhere, but it was over.

Later he told her he'd been tripping on acid.

The next day, Kitty went with a group of people to the coast in Conrad's car. They took LSD and sat on a beach of little black stones, smoothed by the ocean and hot in the sun. Kitty rolled around and dug her hands in the pebbles. She threw them in the air and felt them fall on her legs and stomach like fat, warm raindrops on the surface of a pond. She wandered down the shoreline and sat for a long time, watching the surf churn, until she noticed the tide coming in. She was unsure for a moment how fast it was moving. It suddenly came to her that she would be trapped in her isolated cove if she didn't get back to the others. The cliff behind her, she saw, was steep and greasy — too slick to climb. She began running and didn't stop until she reached Conrad and lay next to him on the pebbles. *I have a lover*, she told herself.

Conrad lived in a big group house up the hill from the campus. It was boxy and white, and they called it "The Westinghouse" because it looked like a dryer. The common rooms were decorated with trash-picked couches and shopping carts. A smell of ether drifted up from the basement, where Conrad made drugs that Kitty had never heard of: MDA, DMT, bromomescaline. She felt brave and tried everything. They went to the movies tripping, or to video arcades, or just wandered around the mall. Conrad smuggled sodium out of the lab at school, and they threw chunks into the Willamette. It exploded on the surface in yellows and oranges, like waterborne fireworks.

They went out late at night in search of food. Their favorite place was a diner downtown where the waitresses had gingham uniforms. One waitress wore a stiff yellow wig and only had teeth on one side of her mouth. She recited the litany of pies on request:

"PeachappleDutchapplecherryblueberrypecanstrawberry rhubarbpumpkinbananacreamBostoncreamlemonmeringue."

"What was that third one?" Conrad would ask, winking at Kitty across a table of half-eaten food.

It was Conrad who suggested she move into the Westinghouse when the room next to his opened up. The first night he stayed with her, and the next night he didn't. The night after that, he still wasn't home when she finally fell asleep. It bothered her, but she kept it to herself. After all, he had never said they were a couple. "It'll be convenient" was all he'd said. A few times she crept abjectly into his room without being invited. She craved him, but she always left him still craving.

Kitty turned her recriminations inward when she came home and found Conrad on the living room couch with someone on his lap—a girl named Holly, who'd hitchhiked up from Eugene in her bare feet. Later that night, after Kitty sneaked downstairs and confirmed that Holly was not sleeping on the couch, she lay awake in her room and imagined them on the other side of the wall: Conrad's hand moving over Holly's shoulder and into the dip of her waist, across her belly, between her legs.

Holly did not leave the next day, as had been her plan. She stayed for weeks. Kitty's pride dictated that she be nonchalant. She, Holly, and Conrad went together to Sodium Beach, and to the diner with the gingham-wearing waitresses. She let Holly pull her hair into a French braid and walked around campus with her and was bitterly relieved when she moved on.

One day, Kitty woke feeling sick and decided to skip her morning lecture. It was afternoon when she got up again, and she was hungry and lightheaded, so she took some Spaghetti-Os off Conrad's shelf and ate them out of the can. A sudden thirst for orange juice came over her. She put a coat on over her flannel nightgown and walked to the Thriftway, where the bright lights and the muzak hit her like a wave. Before she felt it coming, she'd vomited Spaghetti-Os all over the waxed linoleum tiles.

When Conrad found her in bed later that afternoon, she told him about the Spaghetti-Os, and throwing up at Thriftway. "Feel my forehead," she said. "Am I hot?"

"No," he said, climbing in next to her. He reached under her quilt for a breast.

"Ow."

"That hurts?"

"Yeah. Ow, don't touch them."

"Hmm. You didn't miss your period, did you?"

"I don't know," she said. "I don't really keep track." She considered for a moment. "I don't remember having one last month."

"Well, there you go," he said. "C'mon. You can't get any more pregnant." He pulled her nightgown up. "Don't worry — I won't touch your tits."

It was the last time she had sex with Conrad. She woke the next day and found she couldn't stand him anymore. She didn't tell him when she confirmed her condition. She didn't want to give him the satisfaction of knowing something so consequential had come of their adventures.

Kitty skipped the last lecture of the semester and took a bus to the clinic. A small group of protesters lined the sidewalk outside, but they didn't look at her or even pick up their signs as she walked past them. Inside, she changed into a gown and accepted a Valium from the nurse. She worried that it wouldn't work, that somehow all the DMT and LSD and MDA she'd taken in the last few months would neutralize it, but after a few minutes a drowsy feeling came over her. The rest she met calmly: the donut of fluorescent light, the stirrups, the doctor with the port wine birthmark on his cheek, the sucking sound of his machine and the cramping pain. She tried to think about what was happening but she couldn't hold it in her mind.

She told her roommates they would have to get someone else, that she wasn't coming back after winter break, and packed up her trunk and her suitcase and a cardboard box of books. She didn't even own the mattress she'd been sleeping on. After paying for the abortion and losing her security deposit, she was lucky to find something she could afford: the basement room in the house on the cul-de-sac, with its Astroturf and bad lighting and its damp chill that reminded her every day of hard-won self-sufficiency.

After the break and the three weeks of torpor and Jack Benny reruns, Kitty came back to Portland ready to start again. She stayed away from the Student Union and anywhere else she was likely to run into Conrad, and went to work on her incompletes. She was downtown, browsing the table of Reed course books at Powell's, when she saw Jim Frank for the second time. He seemed genuinely pleased to see her.

"You didn't end up going to California?" she asked.

"No, not yet," he said. "I think I will, though, sometime soon, but I just got a job at the 7-Eleven on 28th Street. I'm living on Hawthorne, in my own, my very own apartment. Listen, I'm going to Singles Going Steady now."

Singles Going Steady turned out to be a record store across the street. Inside, they paused for a moment. "You know, you look like a Shangri-La," Jim said. "That is, you look like one of girls in the Shangri-Las. I'll show you."

She followed him to the Oldies section and stood by while

he flipped through a bin, frowning. He pulled a record. On the cover, three girls posed in matching outfits.

"Mary Weiss—the lead singer." He pointed to the one in the middle. "It's your hair, the way you have it parted. That and those kind of pants."

"Pedal pushers."

He looked up at her with surprise. "That is such a good word! Pedal pushers! And your name, too: Kitty. 'It's Kitty's turn to cry.' No, wait—Judy. It's Judy's Turn to Cry."

"Is that one of their songs?"

"No, that's Leslie Gore," he said. "But, um, it's a good name. Yeah, you remind me of Mary Weiss: sad and tough like that. A tough, sad teenager."

He led her to the listening station, where he put the record on and fitted the headphones over her ears. She recognized the first song—"Leader of the Pack"—as soon as it started, but Jim quickly picked the needle up and moved it to another track.

This one began with a somber piano figure in a slow waltz time. Three girls, in hushed unison, spoke a single word: *Past.* Then a lone voice took up the recitation in an amplified whisper: tender, but burred with experience and studio reverb and a trace of a New York accent. *Well now, let me tell you about the past. Past is filled with silent joys and broken toys.* Jim watched while Kitty listened to that song and the next, then carefully lifted the headphones.

"Let me buy this for you," he said.

"I don't have a record player."

"I'm going to buy it anyhow, and we can play it at my place."

Jim's building was not like the complexes on 28th Street. It was brick and old, with a wide, dusty hallway that reminded her of her grammar school. Following him into his apartment she peeked at the bedroom, to the left of the entryway. There was nothing inside but a typewriter, sitting on the floor in a sea of scattered pages.

"Is that where you're writing your novel?"

"That's good, that you remembered that," he said. "Yes, the novel."

Kitty wanted to go in and pick up a page and read it, but she stopped herself.

"What's it like, writing a book?"

"I don't really know how to answer that. It's great, I guess."

There was no furniture in the living room either, except for a rug with a sleeping bag on it and a boombox and a lift-and-play record player. Next to the sleeping bag a picture, torn out of a magazine, was taped to the wall. Kitty bent forward to look: a girl with short hair and thick false eyelashes in black tights and a T-shirt, posing atop an expensive-looking leather footstool shaped like a rhinoceros. Her arms were gracefully outstretched with one leg extended behind her.

"That's Edie Sedgwick," Jim said.

"Who?"

"From the Factory."

"What factory?"

"Andy Warhol's Factory."

"Oh." Kitty had heard of Andy Warhol but she didn't understand the part about a factory.

Still wearing their coats, they sat down on the floor across from each other, each leaning against a wall, and Jim put on the Shangri-Las. The record had an echoey sound to it, as if it had been made specifically to be listened to in a room like this: a cold room with no furniture. The tough, sad girls were Out in the Street, they were Walking in the Sand, they could Never Go Home Anymore. It was dark when the record ended, but Jim didn't turn on the light. Kitty had a strong desire to tell him about Conrad and Holly and the abortion, and about how she was worried that she still felt some pain from it. But she could sense that he would not want her to, so instead she talked about Western Mystical Philosophy and how, now that she'd finally started to do the reading, she felt like everything related to it—even the record they'd just listened to.

"Relates how?" he asked.

"Well, like, Plotinus. I read this thing last night that keeps going through my head: 'The soul, different from the divinity but sprung from it, must needs love.'"

Jim exhaled. "Yeah, that's great, just all by itself. I don't even want to know what it means or where it comes from, you know? Sometimes I'll just open up a book in the middle and get some great phrase, or a good, technical-sounding word that I can drop into my novel somewhere. That's where my head's at."

Later, in the hallway, it occurred to her why the picture of the girl in the black tights had been taped to the wall, at that height, by the sleeping bag.

The next time she was at the library, she remembered what Jim had said, and she looked up *The Thief's Journal*—the book she'd checked out for him in September. She opened it up at random and read.

> *Picturing the world outside, its shapelessness and confusion even more perfect at night, I turned it into a godhead of which I was not only the cherished pretext, object of so much care and caution, chosen and superlatively led despite ordeals that were painful and exhausting to the point of despair, but also the sole purpose of so many labors.*

Kitty started dropping in on Jim at the 7-Eleven when she stayed late at the library. Sometimes, if she was at home in the evening, he would come by her house and they would wander around for a while until he had to go to work. They walked along the median strip of Powell Boulevard, past vast, sparsely stocked thrift stores. They watched some firemen put out a practice blaze in a hollow cement structure in the middle of an asphalt lot. The factories by the river were dark and quiet, except for a few that glowed with swing-shift lights, their exhaust fans humming in the night. Mostly, Jim and Kitty walked through wet, foggy emptiness. Portland was a lonely city, a place where drifters reached the edge of the continent. Jim showed her a hobo camp under the Burnside Bridge near the downtown soup kitchens.

Once, they went to the diner with the pies and saw the waitress who only had teeth on one side of her mouth. Afterward, walking home, Kitty started to tell Jim about Conrad. He looked straight ahead while she spoke, nodding, but he stopped her before she got to the Spaghetti-Os and what came next.

"I want to tell you something, Kitty," he said. "This is important. Any guy will fuck you if you ask. Don't ever worry about that."

The milder weather came. Kitty saw Conrad around, and her other old roommates from the Westinghouse. It would have been impossible to avoid them entirely. She made a point of being friendly but she still kept away from the Student Union. She got a B on her paper for Western Mystical Philosophy, reduced to a C for lateness. That was okay—she'd cleared up the incomplete. It was a struggle, but she was keeping up with all her current classes. Thucydides and Herodotus were still giving her problems, though.

And something else: she still had pain. It had moved upward, spread out, gotten duller. When Tylenol didn't help, she stayed in bed with Windex and a hot water bottle. She knew she should make another appointment at the Women's Health

Center, but she remembered the morning at the clinic and the doctor with the port wine birthmark, and she kept putting it off.

She was at home under her electric blanket when Jim knocked on the basement entrance. The bright April sun blinded her for a minute when she opened the door.

"It's really dark in here," he said. "You should change those bulbs." The other fluorescent light tube had started to burn out, and now they were both strobing.

"What are you doing up so early?" she asked.

"I wanted to bring you some things on my way out of town."

Kitty's stomach dropped.

"Where are you going?"

"California. My sister said I could stay in her garage. In Mountain View."

"But—when are you leaving?" She hoped she didn't sound whiny.

"Now," he said. "Well, tonight. I wanted you to have this." He gave her a thick manila envelope on which he had written, in large block letters, "Real Life in California, by Jim Frank."

"Your novel?"

"Almost." His shoulders went back a little when he said it. "I'll send you the rest when it's finished. And I wanted to give you this, too, since you don't have a radio."

He had brought her his boombox. She took it from him and set it down on her writing desk. "I didn't know you were going," she said.

Irritation flickered across his face.

"I mean, I forgot," she added. "I forgot you said that."

"Here's my address." He'd written it down for her. "And my sister's phone number. But don't give that to anyone. And don't show anyone my novel."

"I don't have a phone," she said. "Write to me, okay?"

"Isn't there one upstairs?"

"No. Well, yes, but it's not mine. I don't use it." She had stopped paying her share of the phone bill. "Okay. Bye, I guess," she said, anxious for him to leave. She felt tears coming and she didn't want him to see them.

She let herself cry for a while after he left. When she was done, she plugged in the boombox and played with the antenna, but the only station she could get through the thick basement walls was a sports talk show. Then she noticed a cassette in the tape player and hit play. For a moment it was just hiss and guitar feedback and thick bass notes dragging a beat. Then the voice came in: male, angry, but as naked and sad as Mary Weiss's. *Turn away, turn away from the wall. Face me now. Face me now.* She took the tape out and looked at it. The label said "FLIPPER," in Jim's handwriting. She put it back in and hit play again. *Show me, show me all your tears. Your pain, your pain makes me burn.*

She opened up the manila envelope and began reading. Someone was driving around in a van looking for someone else. She didn't understand it, but she felt like she was being shown something almost unbearably intimate. She realized she was shivering.

I saw you, I saw you shine.

When the tape ended, she put Jim's novel down. Now her face was burning. She went upstairs and found a thermometer and took her temperature.

The fever went away, but after a few days it came back stronger than before. She was home from school when Jim's first letter came. He had typed all across the back of the envelope. "I am now the only, sole, exclusive warehouseman at a furniture store," he said. "I make $5.65 an hour." He described his sister's garage, and said he was going to buy a car from her neighbor when he got his first paycheck—a 1968 Plymouth Valiant. Gray. The envelope itself was empty.

Kitty kept the thermometer by her bed, more out of curiosity than anything else. She stayed in her nightgown all week while her fever spiked and abated and spiked again. The pain was intense at times, but listening to Jim's cassette tape helped. The sound traveled over a secret frequency, from a different basement room in a place she'd never seen. The hum of the bass and the cymbal's tinny crash answered the dull and sharp sensations in her abdomen and organized them into a kind of music. On one song—a long one that she played over and over—the synthesizer dropped notes around her like falling stars.

Mail came every day. Jim sent lyrics, dreams, a letter to Dear Abby that he had copied out in his own handwriting. She burned with fever while she read them. Sometimes the words ran together and re-formed into other words. At the beginning of the second week, she got a letter in response to one she had sent, apparently, answering questions she didn't remember asking. "There are several schools of thought as to what the last word of "Real Life in California" will be," he wrote. "A note exists in which I determined to end with the word "Oh," which is used throughout the book to denote moments of special grief—just that word on its own. Oh." He said he had borrowed money against his first check and bought the Valiant, and that he was tuning it up. He said he thought she would like California.

Later she remembered standing in the kitchen, talking to Windex. "Oh Kitty," the little gray cat said. "You're moribund."

"What does that mean?" she asked.

And then she was being helped into an ambulance. A roommate had found her passed out on the kitchen floor. At the hospital, a nurse said they were going to test her blood pressure lying down and then sitting up. Kitty watched the cuff inflate and dimly felt it tighten around her arm.

"Good news," the nurse said. "You don't have to sit up." She put an IV needle in the back of Kitty's wrist and taped it down.

"Pelvic inflammatory disease," explained the doctor sitting by Kitty's bed. He clasped his soft, pudgy hands in his lap. A crucifix hung on the wall behind him. Kitty imagined an assembly line: factory workers in hairnets nailing little Christs to their crosses. The bed next to her was empty. Someone—one of her roommates, probably—had brought her some things: pens and a notebook and Jim's boombox.

"You'll need to stay here for at least four or five days," the pudgy doctor was saying, "so we can give you antibiotics and fluid. You were very dehydrated." He stood up. "You should be feeling a lot livelier in a day or two."

"Can you plug that in before you go?" She pointed at the boombox. "And close the door?"

When she was alone, she pressed play and listened for a minute with her eyes closed, waiting to see if the tape worked on her like it had under the heavy blanket of fever, then picked up the notebook and started a letter.

"How is the Valiant running?" she wrote. "Come get me."

The Searchlite

Kitty stood across the street from the Searchlite Lounge on Western and Fountain, just north of the 101 freeway. It didn't look like much from the outside: torn cloth awning, soot-stained facade of imitation stone, a single barred window high up on the front wall. The door was propped open, but with the late afternoon sun backlighting the building she couldn't see inside. She missed the type of bar she'd hung out in back east— taprooms with threadbare pool tables where you could settle in and get comfortable and chew the fat with the neighborhood rummies. People she met here, misunderstanding, kept directing her to places that looked promising but turned out to be imitations: fake English pubs, retro martini lounges.

Her eyes were still adjusting to Los Angeles. She drove down legendary-sounding boulevards—Wilshire, Beverly, La Cienega—sweating into her vinyl car seat, impatient for the city to reveal its glamour. Sometimes as she drove, she spoke to herself in imaginary Raymond Chandler prose: "I followed the Nash west on Sunset and swung up Sepulveda, climbing until I lost his taillights in the fog." She drove on and on, until she realized what should have been obvious from the start: vastness and anonymity were not impediments to her understanding of Los Angeles; they were the essence of the city. Once she accepted that, she started to notice things like the hand-painted Clorox and Palmolive bottles on the sides of Mexican markets, or the little fruit salad carts you saw at certain intersections, or sometimes, late at night, a coyote standing in the middle of a quiet side street.

At a party a few weeks earlier, Kitty had found herself in the garden, one of those backyard shangri-las with Malibu lights and fan palms, in conversation with a man about her age. Like her, he had moved to Los Angeles from the northeast.

"I've been here for almost ten years now," he said when she asked.

"Do you miss New York?"

He shrugged as though the question were irrelevant. "How about you? How long?"

"A little over six months. I moved for a software job."

"And?"

"It's apocalyptic, isn't it?" she said cautiously. "It's beautiful." He smiled in recognition. The flame from the citronella torch flickered in the lenses of his thick-framed glasses. "To tell you the truth, the thing I miss most about Philadelphia is the bars. Regular neighborhood bars."

He nodded, took out a pocket-sized notepad and a pen, and began writing. "Here are some places I think you should check out." He tore off a sheet and handed it to her. "I'm sorry I can't stay and talk more." He had filled both sides of the page with a list of bars and their cross streets—mostly in East Hollywood, though a few had what looked like Skid Row addresses. He'd also written down his phone number, and a note: "Call me if you want a copilot.—Anton."

Something about his air of authority put Kitty off, but she tucked the paper in her wallet anyhow. Later she kept noticing bars from his list, like the Escape Room, or One-Eyed Jack's on Beverly, or the Monte Carlo across from the Ralphs supermarket on Third and Vermont: such a generic sign that it had been invisible to her before. Or the Searchlite Lounge, which was just around the corner from her apartment on Fountain, and which she'd driven past hundreds of times on her way to and from the freeway until finally, today, curiosity overtook her.

Kitty crossed Western and ducked in out of the glare. There were a few men in Carhartts sitting at the bar. An older Asian woman stood behind it, wiping a glass with a rag. No one looked up when she came in. They were all absorbed in a soccer game on the television. She sat on the last stool and ordered a beer. The room was small and seemed smaller because of the low ceiling, which, now that her eyes had adjusted, she saw was covered with what looked like black plastic trash bags. There was no decor to speak of. It looked like a good enough perch: a workingman's bar. The kind of place that, if it were in South Philly, would have glass brick windows, and a jar of pickled eggs by the cash register, and penny tiles in the toilet. She pulled a book out of her bag and settled in.

When she looked up again, a streetlight was buzzing outside the high window. She turned around on her stool and saw three new customers at a small table on the other side of the room. They were trashy-looking. Actually, they looked like hookers: shortie jackets, stripper heels, crotch-high skirts. They sat on the edges of their chairs, legs crossed high, smoking busily. On second glance, Kitty saw that they not women but transvestites. Of course, she thought, they must have come from Santa Monica Boulevard, a block down Western. She'd seen the trannies out at night, and even sometimes during the day: staking out the wide sidewalk, standing in groups under building overhangs, working their way out into traffic.

Kitty signaled to the bartender for another beer. The soccer game had ended or been abandoned, and the jukebox came on. More girls arrived and hopped from table to table, talking loudly in Spanish and English, dancing in place, snapping open compacts to fix their make-up. A girl in an orange fur jacket squeezed her slim hips between two of the men sitting near Kitty and leaned across the bar. Squealing, she slapped one of the men's hands off her ass.

"You ain't paid for that yet, honey," she teased.

"How 'bout I buy you a drink and put my hand in your dress?"

"How 'bout he buy my friend a drink?" She jerked her head back at the man on her other side. "Se siente sola por allá."

Suddenly, Kitty wished there were someone here to share this with. She thought about calling Cathy, the woman whose cubicle was across the aisle from hers. They sometimes had coffee together. Cathy had invited her out for drinks after work a few times, and she'd never reciprocated. But she thought of Cathy's sweater sets, and the framed photos of her husband and kids that she kept on her desk. No, she wouldn't appreciate this scene at all. Then she remembered Anton in the garden, the shadow of the fan palm and the glow of the torch, and how he'd smiled at her word, "apocalyptic." She took his list out of her wallet and dialed the phone number he'd written down, hesitating for a second before hitting Send. She was relieved when she got his voicemail, and considered hanging up.

"Hi, it's Kitty," she said. "From Philadelphia. I'm at the Searchlite now if you want to come by."

The man sitting next to her got up while she was typing. She caught a whiff of floral perfume as someone sat down in his place. In the mirror behind the bar she saw a black Cleopatra wig and a green dress with three-quarter length sleeves. Glancing down, she saw matching green pumps. Her new neighbor sat attentively, hands resting on a pocket book, also green, on the bar in front of her—as though she were at the doctor's office waiting for the receptionist to call her name.

"What you want?" asked the bartender on her next pass.

"A cosmopolitan?" said the transvestite. Her voice strained for an unnatural sweetness.

The drink arrived in a plastic tumbler. When she looked up with obvious disappointment, her eyes met Kitty's in the mirror.

"I guess you have to ask for one of them glasses," she said.

Kitty smiled politely though, she hoped, not invitingly. She craned around to keep tabs on the girl in the orange jacket, but she'd lost the thread of that conversation.

"I'm sorry, go on back to your book if you want," her neighbor said.

"It's too dark to read in here anyhow." Kitty might have been able to hide behind her book indefinitely as a cover for eavesdropping, but it was useless now, so she put it away.

"It's nice, though," the transvestite said, looking around her. Some of the others had made only token efforts at crossdressing. The girl leaning against the jukebox, for instance, was wearing jeans and high-top sneakers, and her hairstyle could have been a boy's cut, but the fit of her jeans and her cap-sleeved blouse signified loudly enough to compensate. She and the others moved and smoked and laughed like they knew they were girls. Looking at the person sitting next to her, who had dressed so carefully, Kitty could only think of a man. Kitty was certain that she hadn't come in with the others, or spent any time on Santa Monica Boulevard. She seemed completely out of place.

"So, is this your first time here?" she asked. The question sounded more personal than she had intended.

"Oh. Yes it is. I drove by and looked before, but, this is the first time I ever came in. What about you?"

"Same as you. I drive past all the time, but I never came in." She extended her hand. "I'm Kitty."

"Janice. Can I tell you something?"

"Of course."

She leaned in conspiratorially. "This is my first time."

"You said that."

"No, I mean my first time," Janice said, waving her hand over her dress. "My first time out." Kitty saw now that she was young—though perhaps she looked younger than she was. She had a round, soft face, and she'd overshot her mouth slightly with dark lipstick. Her foundation stopped in a line at the base of her throat. She'd attempted a languorous, feline sweep in the application of her eyeliner. Her light-colored eyes searched Kitty's face myopically.

"Well," Kitty said, "you look very pretty."

Janice beamed. "Can you watch my drink?" she asked, sliding off her stool. "I have to go to the john." She felt behind her thighs for the hem of her dress to make sure it was in place and walked carefully across the room, pausing for a second before disappearing into the ladies' room.

Janice's expression was full of news when she rejoined Kitty at the bar. "Did you know that they don't have doors on the stalls?"

"I guess so no one does anything illegal."

She considered this silently for a moment. "Shalimar used to come here," she said.

Shalimar. It sounded familiar. Kitty searched her mental inventory of one-named pop singers.

"Wait," Janice said, "I'll show you." She opened her purse and took out her billfold. Kitty peeked at the driver's license showing through the little plastic window—glasses and short brown hair. She produced a much-folded clipping from the *LA Weekly.*

What happened to Atisone Seiuli? read the headline. There was a picture of a dark-haired girl posing on a bedspread in a black bra and panties. Kitty began reading. On the morning of April 22, a woman walking her dog found the body of Atisone Seiuli, clad only in lingerie, on a sidewalk outside Seiuli's Hollywood apartment building.

Kitty skimmed the rest of the article. Atisone Seiuli, a.k.a. Shalimar, was the prostitute Eddie Murphy had been caught with back in 1997—a pre-operative transsexual. That must be why the name rang a bell. Kitty remembered the mug shot in the supermarket tabloids and the snarky jokes on David Letterman. Apparently, Shalimar enjoyed a brief local celebrity after her arrest, then fell to her death from the roof of her apartment building a year later.

"Did you know her?"

"Oh, no," said Janice, refolding the clipping carefully. "I was only sixteen when she died. But it says in there that she used to come to the Searchlite Lounge."

Now Kitty understood: Janice had chosen the Searchlite for her debut because of Shalimar. This article, basically a clipping from the police blotter, was her map of the stars.

"She was from Samoa," Janice continued. "That's why she's so exotic. You know, she was the captain of her cheerleading squad in high school. In Samoa."

"Really?"

"They would have dragged her up and down the football field by her hair at Van Nuys High. Hey, let me get you a drink." Janice waved at the bartender and pointed back and forth between Kitty's empty bottle and her plastic cup. When the bartender turned away, she said, "Shoot, I forgot to ask for a nice glass again."

Taking the first gulp of her beer, Kitty remembered that she hadn't eaten dinner. She was starting to feel a little drunk. The music had grown steadily louder and her throat was getting hoarse from talking over the jukebox.

"I need to eat something," she said.

They leaned against the wall of a 99 Cent Only store, eating fish tacos from a truck parked near the 101 overpass on Santa Monica Boulevard. After Janice bought her a beer, Kitty had felt obliged to invite her along. They'd walked slowly so that

Janice, wobbly on her heels, could keep up. It had clouded over and rained a little while they were in the bar, releasing an ionic, improbably fresh scent into the night air. Kitty could hear the slap of wet tires on the freeway beneath them. A police cruiser nosed onto the Boulevard and drove past slowly.

"My dad's LAPD," said Janice. "If he saw me out here, he'd throw me out of the house for good."

So Janice lived at home. Kitty imagined her hiding in her bedroom, painting on eyebrows and then frantically wiping them off at the sound of her father's cruiser in the driveway.

"Your dad's a cop?"

"Yeah."

"What do you do?"

"I work at my brother's truck-washing shop. But he only gives me part-time."

Kitty looked up the block to see if she recognized any of the trannies gathered around the bus shelter across Western. She tried to picture clumsy, moon-faced Janice working the corner with them. Really, she had no idea what Janice wanted. Was it just to sit in a bar wearing a dress and drinking a cocktail she'd learned about on a television show? For all she knew, Janice might have a bold secret life, performing anonymous sex acts in the public toilets of Van Nuys. Maybe what she wanted was exposure—for her father to catch her out here and banish her for good.

On their way back to the bar, Janice caught her heel in a storm grate. She grabbed for Kitty but missed, and she ended up in a sitting position on the high curb.

"Are you okay?" Kitty asked, reaching down.

"I shouldn't have been walking around without my glasses on." She tried to stand up, then skipped sideways, supporting herself on Kitty's arm. "Oh," she said, "I broke my shoe." She lifted her foot, and the heel dangled. Kitty saw that she was wearing pantyhose, which struck her, for some reason, as almost unbearably sad.

"Look," she said, "I just live a few blocks away."

Janice followed Kitty up the exterior stairs to the apartment, pulling herself along by the railing and hopping on her good shoe. "I know that smell," she said, sniffing at the air. "What is it?"

"Peppercorn." Kitty pointed to a massive tree, the only thing growing in the dirt-lined courtyard. Its delicately filigreed leaves drooped like willow branches, and the ground underneath was littered with pink and white berries. The fragrance followed them inside.

It was still winter back in Philadelphia, but the weather here had become mild already, and Kitty had left the window overlooking the courtyard open. As they walked into the apartment, the repeating tones of a car alarm started up—Whoop! Whoop! Whoop! Whoop! BeeBEE, beeBEE, beeBEE; WEE-uh WEE-uh. Kitty pulled the window shut. "That'll go on for hours," she said.

"Is it coming from your driveway?"

"Believe it or not, it's a bird—a mockingbird, I think. It showed up in the peppercorn tree a few weeks ago. Which, you know, doesn't bother me as much as a real car alarm would. You kind of have to admire the damn thing."

Janice sat on the couch while Kitty went in the other room and rummaged through the pile of shoes on the floor of her closet, trying to find something she would like.

"Is this your family?" Janice called out.

"On the end table? The guy with the moustache and the two little kids?"

"Yeah."

"That's me and my brother and our dad. They're both back in Cambridge."

"What does he do?"

"My dad? He teaches college."

"You-all get along?"

Kitty had talked to her father that morning. She missed him terribly, and her brother, too. He was planning to come out after his semester ended. She looked forward to showing him all the things she'd discovered out here already. Alpine Village, Eaton Canyon, the Western Exterminator sign on Temple, the terrazzo sidewalks downtown, the old cafeteria that was decorated with redwood murals and dusty taxidermy.

"He's okay," she said.

Most of her shoes were plain and utilitarian: sneakers, work boots, job-interview loafers; none of these would do. She had a pair of strappy heels in here somewhere that she'd bought for the office Christmas party. And then she remembered that, of course, none of her shoes were going to fit, because Janice was a man, with man-sized feet. She found a pair of sandals and adjusted the buckles as far as they would go.

"I'm sorry," she said, offering them to Janice. "These are kind of ugly, but see if you can get them on."

Janice wedged a sandal onto her right foot. When she stood up, her heel hung off the end.

Kitty's phone beeped inside her pocket. She dug it out and saw she'd missed a call from Anton. She'd forgotten all about him. Watching Janice straighten her wig and check her lipstick in the mirror by the door, Kitty thought of the journey she'd made that evening: over the Cahuenga Pass and down into East Hollywood, where the beautiful Shalimar had met her doom on a streetlit sidewalk.

Janice hesitated outside the bar, suddenly embarrassed about her shoes.

"See how crowded it is?" Kitty said, opening the door a little so she could peek inside. "No one's going to notice your feet."

The room was packed now. A haze of cigarette smoke hung over the bar. The music was louder, and the voices competing with it had multiplied in the last hour. Scanning the room for familiar faces, Kitty spotted Anton, who had staked out a table in the corner next to the jukebox. He stood up when they came over and caught Kitty off-guard with a cheek-grazing double kiss. Donna Summer moaned orgasmically.

"Anton, this is Janice," yelled Kitty, "Janice, Anton."

He took Janice's hand and kissed it. Kitty saw that the seam under her right arm had split a little.

"Will you excuse me?" Janice said, "I have to go to the ladies'."

"Your friend is a vision," Anton said when she'd gone. His eyes twinkled. "Did you pick her up on the Boulevard?"

"She's from Van Nuys," Kitty said, but he wasn't listening.

"What do you think of the Searchlite?" He gestured magnanimously across the room, as though the scene were something he had invented for her delight.

"I think we're tourists," she said, realizing her mistake. She considered her options. She didn't want to abandon Janice, but then she wasn't sure she was needed, or even relevant. "Will you excuse me? I have to go to the ladies', too."

Just as she turned away from him, the front door banged open. For a moment nothing else changed: Donna Summer kept moaning. The girl in the orange fur jacket kept shimmying with her back to the door. Then a wedge of uniformed cops streamed in. The jukebox went dead, and all Kitty could hear was trannies screaming and cops yelling.

"Against the back wall, hands out, everyone hands out!"

Cops were pulling girls out of the bathrooms and swarming behind the bar. When the lights came on, Kitty saw the cap-sleeved girl with the hi-top sneakers on the ground, a cop pressing her face into the muddy floor and twisting her arm behind her back. Another cop braced his foot against the threshold of the ladies' room and yanked Janice out by both wrists. She made a break for the door, her eyes wide with fear or excitement, but he grabbed her by her waist and threw her against the back wall.

"Hands," he yelled, "hands!" as he dumped the contents of her pocketbook on the floor.

Anton and Kitty stood behind their table, ignored in the chaos. Finally, a cop came over and, despite the bright overhead lights, shined his flashlight over their faces.

"IDs out," he said.

Kitty gave the cop her license. He passed his beam over it and handed it back. Anton dropped his wallet. When he stooped down to pick it up, his glasses fell off.

"It's okay," the cop said, holding up his hand. "You're both free to go."

Anton didn't call her, and she didn't call him, though she eventually went through his whole list. At the Escape Room she met a woman named Diane who lived upstairs in the Kipling Arms. One-Eyed Jack's was inexplicably closed on a Thursday night the first time she stopped by, but the next time she found it open and sat at the bar—a big square corral in the middle of a cement room. An old lady, mistaking the stranger on the next stool for Kitty's date, tried to get him to buy her a rose.

The Monte Carlo had a pool table. She shot a game of eight ball with a guy who was painting buildings that stood in all the places where Charles Bukowski had once lived. He showed her snapshots he'd taken of a Pollo Loco on Vermont and a blood lab on Hollywood Boulevard. "Right where we are standing," he told her, "was a boarding house run by a Filipino man, and that man was Bukowski's landlord." She told him his reverence was misplaced.

When she drove past the Searchlite, she sometimes thought she saw a familiar face among the girls smoking cigarettes on the sidewalk, but she didn't see Janice. Janice was back in Van Nuys at her father's house, or she was washing trucks, or she was somewhere else in the city of night.

FOOD & BEVERAGE

The Breakfast Shift

I spent my twenties leaning over the classified section of the *Globe*, pencil in hand. Actually, though, I only ever got one job from the Help Wanteds: waiting tables at a greasy spoon over by Boston City Hospital. I reported to the address on Washington Street without expectation and filled out an application at the faux Fifties counter. I was so accustomed by then to thinking of myself as unemployable that I was shocked when the manager, a rheumy-eyed drunk with a thinning white pompadour, hired me on the spot for the breakfast shift. He told me to come back in the morning, and then he didn't seem sure who I was when I tapped on the locked glass door at 5:45 a.m.—still half-dreaming but ready to work the six to two-thirty.

Recession, a lack of ambition, and vague artistic leanings had stranded me in a low-grade bohemian funk, and it felt good to have somewhere to be for a change. My bicycle commute— through banks of vaporous streetlight, past the wet sidewalks and dark doorways of the deserted pre-dawn South End—felt spooky and glamorous, like I'd fetched up in a strange city. No one I knew went to bed at nine p.m. Friends, confused by my new schedule, stopped calling for fear of waking me up. A beer after work now meant drinking at 2:30 in the afternoon, which meant drinking with people who drink at 2:30 in the afternoon, which in turn put me in specialized company. The combined effect was, for a while, pleasantly dissociative.

I never got used to waking up early. Each workday began in a slowly dissipating dream-state: the dark, sleepy passage through empty streets; the arrival at the locked glass door from which spilled the only light on the block; the silent cigarette-and-coffee interlude leaning side-by-side against the counter with Lloyd, the breakfast cook, who was tall and handsome and jet-black, and who, in his white, mushroom-shaped toque, made me think somewhat guiltily of the man on the Cream of Wheat box. Then the rheumy-eyed manager would open up and let in the first customers—usually delivery truck drivers—before passing out on a lawn chair in the stockroom.

With that, the engine of the day turned over, setting in motion the thousand trivial urgencies of waitressing. The delivery drivers ate their eggs and paid their checks, passing on their way out the Boston Edison workers who arrived in groups of three and four, identical in their winter Carhartts, then table-hopped, creating an atmosphere of screwball anarchy. And as I struggled to keep track of their orders, and as they helpfully passed the plates to one another, the sun would rise unnoticed. Then the civilians started coming in and ordering pancakes, and by the time I had a chance to look out the window, the breakfast rush was winding down and my shift was half over. Another cigarette break, and then construction workers from nearby building sites began showing up for their blue-plate specials. Lunch rush, an hour of stragglers, some sidework—refilling ketchup bottles, wrapping silverware in paper napkins—and my workday was done. In the middle of the afternoon, a time of day when I would normally have been drinking Dunkin' Donuts coffee hunched over the Help Wanteds, I would get on my bike and ride home. Or, having put in a full day's work, I might head over to Lou's, a cavernous taproom around the corner where the clientele largely overlapped with ours.

Our customers had nothing to do with Boston City Hospital, although we were practically in its shadow. Even with the pass-through traffic—cabbies and hard hats, artists drifting over from the warehouse district to the east—our greasy spoon, which had only been there for a moment and would be gone a moment later, was a local joint. It surprised me to find that the late-night bar scenes I'd worked as a cocktail waitress, for all their sleazy drama, couldn't touch this place when it came to street theater. Midway through my first shift, an old man slipped on some ice cubes, and I rushed across the room to help him up. He was shaking like a wet sparrow as I steered him to a chair, but before I could sit him down, the manager grabbed his other arm and gave him the bum's rush out the door.

"Guy takes a dive in here every other week," he said off-handedly. "He's got a park-bench lawyer on retainer."

I learned about the change-for-a-twenty short con a few days later. I was filling in for the cashier, ringing someone up at the takeout counter, when a man came in off the street.

"How you doing this morning, Sunshine?"

In fact, he'd caught me in a good mood: a few days under my belt, getting my sea legs, enjoying the brisk, purposeful clack and chime of the cash register. He bought a can of Pepsi, paying with a twenty.

"Say," he said as I counted his change out on the counter, "can I trade in some of these extra ones while you've got the till open? I've got, let's see, fifteen ones and a five . . ."

Lloyd leaned over and slammed the register drawer shut with his spatula.

He was right to keep an eye on me, because I was idiotically smitten by the flimflammers. But the regulars were at least as interesting. There was, for instance, an older black gentleman who wore fastidious tracksuits and drank Earl Grey tea. I would have singled him out in any case for the elegant way he had of angling his chair out from under the table and crossing his long, velour-clad legs; that is, I would have noticed him even there weren't usually a line of people near his table, waiting for an audience with him. I recognized his name when Lloyd spoke it; he was a neighborhood activist who had recently run for mayor. Against every expectation, he'd nearly defeated a well-connected Southie Irish pol—a ham-faced baby kisser apparently sent over from central casting to replace the preceding ham-faced baby kisser. That part of the South End was still a black neighborhood at the time. Though white money had begun its inexorable march up Mass Ave, many of those grand brownstones still sheltered widowers with cardboard suitcases renting furnished rooms by the week. In this part of Boston, the activist might as well have been elected. Like Mayor Curley at his kitchen window, he kept office hours in the back of our restaurant so that the widowers and their landladies and everyone else could petition him for help with wayward children or SSI applications or utility company disputes or civil service exams.

The menu gave a nod to soul food, for which the neighborhood was then still known. We served salty greens shimmering with fat, and sweet potato pie, and you could get grits with your eggs. And then there was all the ham, which I cannot think of without remembering the Hamily: three young black women and a baby who came in almost every morning. One was tall and thin and had a wig like a girl-group bouffant. The other two were very fat. The fatter and younger of them was light-skinned, with smooth red hair and freckles. The baby must have been hers, because it always sat in its car seat on a chair next to her. They ordered ham every morning—ham and eggs, or ham omelets, or just great slabs of ham steak—so we called them "the Hamily." I assumed they were hookers, and probably junkies too, because they drained the entire sugar jar into their coffees every morning. They didn't tip much, usually no more than a few sticky dimes and quarters, but I missed them on the mornings when they didn't come in. And when I spotted one or another of them on the street, it seemed somehow auspicious.

To understand what the Hamily meant to me, it would help if you'd waited on tables. It didn't come naturally. I was, I suppose, competent, but I had to remind myself not to look agitated; to sympathize with someone who'd asked for rye toast and gotten wheat. "It ain't that hard," said Lloyd. "Just do what they say do." Which was only sort of right, because the key to waitressing is not efficiency or stamina or the ability to calculate a six percent meal tax on the fly. Waiting tables, like prostitution, is largely a matter of play-acting. I knew this, but I willfully blew my lines in the scenes we all ran through every morning.

"Why are women like tornadoes?" a cabbie nursing his bottomless cup of coffee at the counter might ask.

"Okay, why?"

"They moan like hell when they come and they take the house when they leave."

In such exchanges I had the options of hilarity and shock, but I was stubborn and usually chose a third way: indifference. If this was received as prudishness or abraded feminist sensibilities (which amounted to the same thing as far as I was concerned), I'd bristle at the idea that I could be offended. Meanwhile, the Hamily gummed their ham slabs serenely, geologically, requiring nothing from me but ham and coffee and a full jar of sugar. Rightly or wrongly, I took them for kindred spirits.

After a while, I was riding to work under a pale sky; then, as spring approached, a weak dawn. Soon it was warm enough to prop open the kitchen door. I'd take my mid-morning cigarette break while Osman, the doleful Turkish prep cook, peeled potatoes, the oud music on his boombox pulsing under the noise of the dishwasher. As soon as weather permitted, the manager abandoned the lawn chair in the stockroom and began napping in his station wagon—a Pontiac Safari that barely fit in the narrow brick alley leading out to Washington Street. From the kitchen door I could see the top of his pompadour lolling on the bench seat. Above, the back wall of the hospital, and the A/C condenser looming over the alley, and beyond that, a patch of sky.

I'd had my doubts about the breakfast shift, but in some ways I found the routine agreeable—even a relief. Where there was no choice there was no anxiety. I stopped looking for meaning in how I spent my time and who I spent it with. What I did was I worked, and the people around me were my co-workers and my customers. That was the meaning of our relationships, and to investigate further was pointless.

Which is not to say I didn't enjoy their company. Sometimes I'd run into the manager or Lloyd or someone else from the greasy spoon at Lou's after work, and we'd sit at the long, curved walnut bar in the watery afternoon light drinking rum and cokes from blue plastic dixie cups. If I stayed around for a second drink I might see a truck driver I'd waited on earlier in the day, or a construction worker or two, or one of the neighborhood people.

One Friday afternoon I stayed late at Lou's, drinking with Lloyd and the manager. As the light faded in the high glass brick windows, our barman stepped out from behind the bar to plug in the jukebox. Until then, I hadn't noticed a jukebox. I'd only known Lou's as a quiet place for afternoon drinking, where the shuffle of bedroom slippers on linoleum could be heard; where conversation competed only with steakhouse commercials on an AM radio, and the echoey clank of empties under a high tin ceiling.

The machine came to life with an a cappella doo-wop intro, its final sad-trombone note resolving into the Spaniels' "Goodnite, Sweetheart, Goodnite." Had this song been queued up when the jukebox was unplugged at closing time? As if propelled by the music, two construction workers got off their stools and headed over to the pool table. One fed the quarter slot, the other racked 'em up. That sound—the tumble of rented pool balls—traveled some neural pathway eroded in my brain by nights of barroom loitering and booth parties . . . all that I was missing on the breakfast shift. I put my two quarters on the rail of the pool table, strolled over to the jukebox, and punched in a few songs. There was some really great stuff on there. I sat between Lloyd and the manager, watching the game, waiting for my turn.

"If you should lo-o-o-ose me, oh yeah . . . you'll lose a good thing," sang Barbara Lynn.

"Who's playing those fine songs?" asked the barman. When I raised my hand, he put a stack of quarters in front of me and said, "Keep 'em coming."

I won my first game on an eight-ball scratch and the next one on a lucky rail shot. Then Lloyd was up, and the manager dragged a stool over to watch us play. Lloyd's game was stealth: deceptively casual, never an easy leave, but I somehow ended up winning that one too, and Lloyd stuck around to coach me as I took on the next guy.

"Bank the ten," he'd say, or "Try the combo."

"Put some English on it," ventured the manager, and Lloyd leaned in and whispered, "It ain't even about that, kitten. You got this one."

A row of quarters appeared on the rail. I've never been better than a fair pool player, but the planets aligned that night, as they sometimes do, and soon I was ruling the table. Lloyd would point at a ball and I'd sink it, as though the pockets were magnetized. Everyone kept giving me money for the jukebox and buying me drinks, and the more rum and cokes I drank, the truer my shots were.

"*Cry, cry baby,*" sang someone named Garnett Mimms, "*Welcome back home.*" In a place like Lou's you can't go wrong playing songs you've heard of by people you haven't.

I don't know how long my winning streak lasted. I exhausted the construction workers, who—like me—had to be up early, and the night customers lined up to take their place. The barman, the cardboard-suitcase bachelors, everyone in the place gathered from the four corners of the bar, all eyes on me. I kept my face immobile for as long as I could, like a pitcher in the middle of a no-hitter. When I looked up from the table at one point, I saw the manager stretched out across a booth seat, snoring.

"Lloyd," I asked, eyeing the low center of the cue ball as I steadied my bridge, "what's your favorite part of the breakfast shift?"

"Favorite how?"

"What's the part that really makes you feel good?"

"Going home, I guess. Don't try to bank it, honey. You can cut it straight in."

"I like the mid-morning cigarette best of all. You know? That buzz you get? Like a virtuous feeling of knowing how long you've been up?"

"Cross-side. Three in the side. "

"And then you ride home, and sometimes you see someone you know from, oh, from before, and it's like you've had an indescribably, unrelatably weird experience and you can't explain it to them."

"You paying attention? He's sneaking up on you."

"Imagine, say, that you've been trapped in an elevator for hours and hours with a talking dog. Lloyd, are you listening? You couldn't believe it at first—I mean, obviously—but after a few hours you get used to it. And then you escape from the elevator finally—like, through a hatch in the ceiling—only to find that the day has just gone on without you."

"No, not the fourteen. That's one of his. You're solids."

"You walk down the street and the rush hour traffic flows past, indifferent to you and your hours of confinement with the talking dog."

"Okay, kangaroo, time for you to hop on home."

"Okay."

"You need a ride?"

"Yes, please."

On Monday, when I tapped on the glass at quarter to six, Lloyd let me in. I saw over his shoulder that Osman, instead of being in the kitchen mixing biscuit batter, was sweeping the floor, ineffectually poking his broom under tables and around chair legs. His cheeks were flushed and his dark-lashed eyes were narrowed, turning his usual expression of philosophical gloom into something else—perhaps anger, or humiliation, or both.

Lloyd met my questioning look with a cocked eyebrow, and then I noticed an unfamiliar man counting bills at the cash register. What had happened here, some sort of audit? This person was dressed for the office, perhaps an office with a casual dress code. He wore large, rimless glasses and a blue striped oxford shirt with the sleeves rolled up. He had a coppery tan, and his hair looked like it was growing out of an expensive cut. The man looked up and walked over to me with his right hand extended.

"Hi!" he said. "I'm Michael. I'm taking over around here as of today. No, not taking over—I'll just be taking on the management duties going forward. But I want you to know that I'll be here with you guys, shoulder to shoulder in the trenches. Like I told Osmond, we're all going to pitch in from now on wherever we're needed. And Osmond, I want *you* to know that no one here is above pushing a broom. Not even me! Excuse me." With that he disappeared into the stockroom.

"Where . . . ?" I looked around for the manager.

"Fired," answered Lloyd. "And watch out for this one. He sneeze with his eyes open."

So began the era of Michael. As promised, he pitched in everywhere. He never stopped moving and always seemed a little overheated. When he mopped his face with a handkerchief you could see a spreading dampness under the arm of his oxford shirt. He ran around making toast and answering the phone and, yes, stabbing frantically at the counter stools with a broom while the cabbies lifted their feet; but he left little piles of sweepings everywhere, and he burned the toast, and his rushing and darting disrupted the coordinated rhythm of movement in the narrow passage between the counter and the grill. He seemed to especially like working the cash register. He would send the cashier to bus tables or do dishes so he could take over. The Hamily, the truck drivers, the slip-and-fall artist, the neighborhood activist: Michael rang them all up with the same impersonal cheer. Then he would disappear into the stockroom, and for a while the pre-Michael equilibrium would return.

When it was slow, and even when it wasn't, Michael was chatty. You might even say he was prone to talking jags. I found out that he had been a lawyer—it was unclear how recently—and that in fact the owner of the greasy spoon had been his client. He said he'd replaced the rheumy-eyed manager "as a favor to the owner" and was vague about the circumstances under which he had stopped practicing law. Embarrassingly, he took a liking to me. He opened up about his recent divorce, how he was petitioning for visitation rights so he could have his son at his condo for sleepovers. Massachusetts family law, he said, was stacked against him. "The father, for all intents and purposes, has fewer rights than a grandparent or even a maternal aunt or uncle," he explained.

He buttonholed me for advice about his kid.

"Just be there for him," I suggested vaguely.

In a moment of weakness I invited him to join me at Lou's after work. I instantly regretted it, but he seemed so grateful for the friendly gesture. Sitting next to him at the bar, I realized that I hadn't seen the old manager there since the night of my winning streak.

Once, Michael's ex-wife came into the restaurant. She walked up to him and said nothing—just held her hand out, palm up, her expression suspended somewhere between disgust and rage. She looked like she might be a lawyer too. You could see lines and hollows of exhaustion under her makeup. Michael, also without saying anything, took a wad of bills out of his front pocket and put it in her hand, and she spun around on her pumps and left. I found that my jaw was clenched in sympathy with hers.

The register started coming up short at closing: ten or twenty dollars here and there, until one night it was a few hundred light. The owner wanted to file a police report, but Michael intervened, and they let the cashier go without getting the cops involved. But money kept disappearing. One of the dinner waitresses got fired, and another cashier. Then one morning I came in to find the owner in the restaurant there, conferring with Michael and Lloyd. Michael said he'd found the stockroom door ajar when he'd opened up. Some cases of canned goods were missing, and some hams, and half a dozen frozen turkeys: obviously an inside job.

This time the owner did call the police. Several hours later, as the breakfast rush was winding down, a cruiser pulled up and double-parked outside the restaurant. Through the glass, we saw the owner and Michael talking to the two cops on the sidewalk. After a few minutes, they came inside and went straight back to the kitchen. I skipped my mid-morning cigarette break in the alley door and sat at the counter instead, watching Lloyd scrape the grill down. Finally I gave up waiting for him to say something.

"Who do you think . . ."

He shook his head, dispelling my question.

The sounds of conversation from the kitchen got louder and more agitated until, just as the early lunch rush was kicking in, Lloyd took off his toque and went back through the swinging doors. Orders started to pile up. The new cashier was plating blue-plate specials as fast as she could.

Finally, Osman emerged from the kitchen in handcuffs, a cop gripping each elbow and the owner trailing them. Osman stared straight ahead, chin up and shoulders square, as they steered him through the lunch crowd, out the front door, and into the back of the cruiser. I went back and saw Lloyd packing up his knives while Michael looked on with an unreadable expression.

"Watch your ass, Kitten," said Lloyd as he brushed past.

After work I found Lloyd at Lou's, as I'd known he would be. We had the place to ourselves except for the barman and, at the other end of the bar, an old man sleeping on his folded arms with his hat sitting on the stool next to him. Lloyd ordered us some rum and cokes. When his change came, he gave me a quarter and said, "Why don't you plug in the box and hit 17A for me one time?" The barman nodded, so I did as he said.

"*If you should lo-o-o-ose me,*" sang Barbara Lynn as I sat down. I looked around, wanting to memorize everything: Lloyd's quiet profile, the blue plastic dixie cups, the corona of dust hovering in the shaft of sunlight over the old man's bald head.

"Well, what do you know about that?" said Lloyd, breaking the silence.

"You don't think Osman—" I remembered him angrily poking his broom around the table legs on the day Michael showed up.

"Oh hell no. You know who took all that shit, and the money too."

"Poor Osman."

"Here's to poor old Osman. And kitten, I wouldn't suggest waiting 'til it come around to you."

"I don't get it, though. What does Michael want with a bunch of hams?"

"He's on the pipe, sweetie. One ham, one rock."

"Crack? No way."

"Don't you smell what come out of that stockroom after take a break?"

I thought about Michael mopping his face with his handkerchief. "But he's a lawyer!"

"Oh brother. Just watch your ass."

I don't know if it was because I'd been tipped off or because things were catching up with him, but it seemed to me that Michael really started to fall apart after Lloyd left. The ballast was gone, I suppose. Michael hired new people to replace all the ones who had gotten fired to cover up his petty, crack-scale embezzling, and then he started churning through the replacements. I thought about inviting him out for another drink, just to shore up my position a little, but I knew I should quit before my turn came.

The end came suddenly for me, as it had for the others, and despite the cloud of inevitability that hung over all of us, it managed to catch me off-guard. I went down to the stockroom looking for coffee filters and found Michael there, absorbed in the task of massaging pipe with flame. Inhaling, he raised his head, and his eyes surged with toxic adrenaline as they met mine. My luck had run out. I walked out the alley door and into the melting August sun, and the next day I slept until ten o'clock.

The Smockey Bar

As is often the case with bartenders, a lot of people knew Smockey a little. Smockey wasn't talkative, he didn't call you "Sport," he betrayed no particular enthusiasm for anything except WWII documentaries on the History Channel, which was always on in his bar. But if you spent enough time there, you learned a few things about him. For instance, his name wasn't really Smockey. That was a sort of stage name that he'd inherited when his father died. Smockey the Elder, a South Philadelphia Italian, had opened up the bar in what was then a Polish neighborhood, so he gave it what he thought was a Polish-sounding name, "The Smockey Bar," and he became Smockey. And when he passed the bar on to his son, he passed the name on too.

I liked the place right away, just based on the sign: black lettering on a white field, the kind of Plexiglas sign that lights up at night, though it was afternoon when I first stopped in. It was on the ground floor of a narrow row house—just wide enough for a long bar and a few small tables and a pay phone. The walls were paneled, stained dark and coated with a glossy spar varnish. I thought at first that a trick of perspective was making the room appear to taper toward the back, but in fact the building wasn't square. It must have been built as an afterthought to fill in the slightly trapezoidal space between two older houses.

Smockey had the place to himself when I first came in—an old man in a vest with a nice full head of Grecian Formula-black hair, brushed straight back from his forehead. He was sitting on a stool by the door and looking out at Passyunk Ave. I sat near the front so he wouldn't have too far to walk.

"A lager, please," I said as he dumped my ashtray and swabbed the bar with a grey dishrag.

"Woant a gleyce?"

"Sorry?"

"A gleyce? Or you just woant the bottle?"

"Oh . . . no glass. Just the bottle is fine."

He fetched himself an O'Douls and went back to his stool, and we sat in companionable silence until a couple of other old guys came in and started chatting me up. I recognized them. I'd seen them sitting in lawn chairs outside the barbershop on 10th Street, a few blocks away. Introductions were made all around, and I stayed for another lager. At some point a kid came in—really a kid, maybe not even in high school—and bought a six-pack to go.

"You know, Smockey," I said when the kid was gone, "I don't think he was twenty-one."

"Bah. He ain't even eighteen," Smockey said.

There was no jukebox at Smockey's, but if there had been, it would have been loaded with Sinatra. The walls were covered with Sinatrabilia: posters, signed photos, even a moody, heavily impastoed oil painting of young Frank leaning against a lamppost. It was that kind of place, an old man's bar. The inner circle of regulars were guys with names like Taffy and Bimbo, old friends from the neighborhood who split their time between the barbershop and a La-Z-Boy when they weren't looking in on Smockey. The place belonged to them, but I think Smockey liked to have young people around, too. There were plenty of other old man bars in the neighborhood—places with the same dark paneling and nicotine stained mirrors and shelves sparsely stocked with Old Granddad bottles and bowling trophies—but the Smockey Bar had a particular geniality that encouraged mixing. Sometimes, later in the evening, every barstool would be occupied, and union plumbers would rub shoulders with bookstore clerks. And as the volume rose from all those minds meeting, Smockey would turn on the closed captioning so he could follow along as the Luftwaffe got its ass kicked in the Battle of Britain.

I started coming in regularly, and he set me up with a tab. Before long he was trying to get me to buy the place off of him.

"Why would I want to do that?" I asked. "You're like a farmer, Smockey. When was the last time you had a day off?"

"She's got you there, Smock," said Taffy.

Smockey probably hadn't had a day off since he started helping his dad out behind the bar when he was ten years old. He himself had no help; he was there seven days a week. If it wasn't busy, he took an hour off in the afternoon to go home for lunch, but otherwise, he made do with whatever he had warming in the ceramic steam well behind the bar: canned chili, beef stew, clam chowder and oyster crackers. He'd never married—he lived with his sister around the corner—and now he was old, and stiff, and he'd heard all Taffy's jokes, and he was ready to retire. He wanted to go fishing. There was a picture of a bass boat taped to the cash register, and a postcard of a beach in Florida. But there was no Smockey III.

It became a routine between us. "When are you gonna take the joint off my hands so I can move to Florida already and get warm for a change?" he'd ask as he plunked a bottle of beer in front of me, and I'd wave him away. But secretly, I fantasized about it. What if I raised the money somehow and took over? Every decision for the rest of my life would be made. I imagined myself sitting on his stool by the window and gazing out at the pizza place across the street, slowly shrinking and desiccating, my hair getting blacker and blacker as I presided over my wedge-shaped time capsule.

Another thing I learned about Smockey: he'd been born upstairs, at a time when working-class Italian women had their children at home. He had probably been taken down to the bar and shown off to his father's customers before he even saw the South Philadelphia sky. One evening I brought someone in with me, and when Smockey went into his routine about unloading the bar, my friend asked for a tour of the upper floors.

"There ain't nothing up there now, but you can go ahead and look," Smockey said.

We found a jukebox on the second floor, and stacks of chairs, and tables too big for the bar downstairs, and a pile of disconnected swag lamps that must have hung over the tables—everything under a blanket of dust. There was a clawfoot tub in the bathroom, left behind after a casual renovation. I imagined young Smockey knocking down the walls of his childhood home, eager to banish the crepuscular gloom of his father's time. I imagined flush years, and couples dancing, and after-hours poker games with Bimbo and Taffy. And I saw how Smockey's world had closed up like a telescope. First he'd left his apartment on the third floor for a clean room at his sister's house. Then the second floor of the bar had become too much, so he'd abandoned that too. Now, finally, he wanted to lock the front door and hand someone else the key.

I moved away to a city where there were no old neighborhoods, or not in any form I could recognize. I drove through permanent sunlight, past endless iterations of the same strip mall, trying to find a bar where I could start up a tab and settle in. After a while, I stopped looking for a Smockey Bar and developed an appreciation for the cinderblock-and-stucco cantinas that were its native counterpart. Word came to me that Smockey had sold the bar. I didn't mourn it, though, because I pictured Smockey with a fishing rod in his hand and a cooler of O'Douls at his side.

And then, not long after that, Smockey died, and someone sent me an obituary—a tribute, really, written by another of his young customers. It was full of surprises. Smockey hadn't moved to Florida. He was still living with his sister when he died. According to the article, he'd never even been farther than New Jersey, and he didn't know how to swim. When he sold the bar, he hadn't bought a bass boat: he'd bought a new Cadillac and parked it over by the barbershop every day, and he'd told anyone who asked that selling the bar was the biggest mistake he ever made.

The Smockey name died with him. The old white sign with the block letters has been replaced by a giant, whimsical Schlitz can. The upstairs room is open for business, and they have music, and quizzo nights. And, in what I guess is a lunkheaded gesture of commemoration, they call it "The Dive."

Tomack

Nancy and I are driving down the Ridge Pike spotting Ladies of Norristown: women with bowl haircuts and nutty eye make-up walking along the side of the road in mismatched footwear. The Pike turns into East Main Street as you approach the business district. Scratch-and-dent appliance stores, astroturfed tax offices, television repair shops. Nancy and I agree: a room above a discount store in Norristown PA is where we picture ourselves once we've exhausted all other possibilities.

An old man in a paper hat dispenses cherry water ice through a window cut out of a plywood storefront. Next to the water ice stand is a nondescript bar, its door propped open to let in the June breeze. We stop in for a glass of beer. There are five or six barflies holding down the fort, and we get a few looks when we sit down. The barman tells us we just missed happy hour, which is funny because it's 3:30 on a Tuesday afternoon.

And now we're waiting out the rush-hour traffic. After a while, a lady of Norristown comes over and tells us they thought we were soliciting when we came in. Nancy reassures her that we aren't, and soon we're all friends. I try, but I can't establish whether they thought we were salesmen or hookers.

Rush hour has come and gone. The old man with the paper hat is here now, and he's showing Nancy a dream book. She's earnestly explaining to him why he shouldn't play the lottery. A number, she says, can never be due. A dream is just a way of talking to yourself. You need to make your peace with the water ice and the plywood window, or if you really want to take your chances, get on a bus for Philadelphia.

The door flies open with a bang. A young man, maybe twenty-four or twenty-five, stands in the doorway with his arms spread in an enveloping gesture. He runs over to the jukebox and dials up a song: "Lovergirl," Teena Marie. He peels off his shirt, takes a running start, and jumps up on the bar. Everyone ignores him as he twists and bends and pumps his fists. Soon, perspiration has pasted his lustrous black hair to the sides of his handsome face. When the song ends he jumps down behind the bar, puts his shirt back on, and holds out his hand to me: "Tomack's the name. T-O-M-A-C-K. What are you girls drinking?"

"The stars are available tonight," I say to Nancy as we stagger past the padlocked plywood water ice window. What I mean is that the dim lights of Main Street are too feeble to reach the starry dome above. Nancy considers this and replies, "I think Tomack used to be my dental hygienist."

Catch of the Day

Pinky's New York Deli is not in New York, and it's not really a deli either. It's a coffee shop in a long, dark room. The chairs scrape unpleasantly on the brown quarry tiles, and the square tables are arranged at an angle so the waitresses can squeeze between them and the Plexiglas-topped half-wall separating the dining room from the kitchen. Under the glass on each tabletop is a cutout of a smiling fish that says, "Catch of the Day." The catch of the day is always chipped beef.

It would be depressing, except that there seems to be a tacit understanding to the contrary between the Pinky's staff and the collection of old ladies and neighborhood johnnies and lunch-hour nurses who cheerfully patronize the place. Really, everything about it seems like communal gesture, an agreement, a temporary installation. It's a restaurant now, but you get a feeling that it could be a travel agency tomorrow, and that yesterday it might have been a shop where an old man in a toupee repaired travel alarm clocks and electric carving knives.

We take our lunches at Pinky's—Suzy, Bob and I. We're working down the street in a vacant row house. There are no windows in the house—just thick, opaque plastic sheeting that heaves in and out like a bellows in the November wind. We wear two layers of long underwear, two pairs of gloves, etc. We had a propane garage heater, but the fumes were giving us headaches, so now we use a little electric space heater. It has a digital readout: 25 degrees, 39 degrees, 46 degrees . . . it usually plateaus there around lunchtime, and we put on yet another layer and run to Pinky's.

On the walls at Pinky's are posters with illustrations of Hollywood legends in iconic settings. There's one of Mount Rushmore where, instead of Washington, Jefferson, Roosevelt, and Lincoln, it's Bogart, Monroe, Dean, and Presley. The theme continues on the menu, because Pinky's is really only a New York deli inasmuch as the sandwiches are named after celebrities. The corned beef on rye is a Stan Laurel, and the grilled chicken is a Hallie Berry, and so on. We parse the menu obsessively. Why is the veggie melt a Woody Allen? Why is the egg salad a Fred Astaire? Sometimes I think I see a pattern. The plain steak hoagie is a Frank Sinatra and the cheese steak hoagie is a Sammy Davis Jr. A minimal pair. But then . . . why is the turkey burger a Lucille Ball while the turkey cheeseburger is a Yul Brenner? We wax Talmudic over our menus and luxuriate in the warmth.

There are two lunchtime waitresses. One is cheerful and pretty and wears her hair in a high ponytail. The other waitress we call the Troll. It's unkind, I know, but there you have it. The Troll is short and powerfully built. Her brown hair is shoulder length but bristle-short on top with a slightly longer fringe across her brow. She has two large rabbit teeth, completely visible even when she's saying "water" or "bulkie roll." The sheer volume of her front teeth seems to muffle her speech. Her eyes are thick-lashed, deep-set, surrounded by bruise-colored rings that remind me of something I heard about people getting black eyes from scuba diving. Her only expression is one of blank surprise.

They usually have a newspaper at the front table—the one where the cook sits on his cigarette breaks. I grab the Lifestyle section on my way in, because I like to do the sudoku. Today, the Troll is our waitress. Suzy orders the chicken rice soup. They make a wonderful chicken soup, with dill and turnips, which you can get with either rice or noodles. Bob orders a

Rock Hudson—that's a cheeseburger—and I go for a soup/half-sand combo, chicken rice with half a Julie Andrews (turkey, Swiss, coleslaw and Russian dressing). When my Julie Andrews comes, I open it up and sprinkle my potato chips on top of the coleslaw. I bite down into the spongy rye and feel the satisfying crunch. I suppose you could say that we are regulars. Who knows what nicknames they have for us?

The front door swings open. Another regular enters, stops up front to pick up what's left of the newspaper, and sits at the table next to us. He is slow-moving, swaddled head to toe in grey and black scraps, carrying his house with him in a duffle bag. He unwinds the shirt that covers his face and stuffs it in his pocket. His right eye is frozen and cataract-clouded, but when he fixes you with his left eye, you can't look away. It is clear, intelligent, impersonal and steady. We call him Odin.

"No one working here gets to tell my soup about rice."

Odin talks to himself constantly in a low voice, almost a whisper. It has a quality, though, that cuts through the layers of white noise, so you pick up words and phrases and sentences almost without realizing it.

" . . . lock you up or knock you up . . . "

Sometimes you aren't sure if it's Odin talking or just some mote of synaptic dust drifting around in your skull.

We stretch out our lunch hour as long as possible. We order coffee refills and quiz each other on the menu until the inevitable can no longer be forestalled. No plumbing in the row house, so we make our final visits to the toilet, which for some reason is as cold as a meat locker. We pass Odin on the way out.

"Tax-deductible piece of shit."

Outside, Bob says, "Did you hear what he called me?" Suzy and I try to distract him. He's quiet all the way back to work, brooding.

At work, we listen to a radio we found in the basement.

It's a tabletop set in a handsome wood-look cabinet—the kind you used to see on the reception desk at the dentist's office. There's a logo next to the speaker: "Eazy 101," topped with a little rainbow. And an on-off button, and a volume knob, but you can't tune it. It only gets one station, which used to be muzak but which is now a lite-rock station called B101—"the Bee." We listen to the Bee all day. It's like a game of Billy Joel chicken. Bob has less stamina than Suzy and I do, and he sometimes finds he has to go work in another part of the house. I've learned that Suzy has a savant-like capacity for remembering song lyrics, and song names, and all kinds of other things she doesn't especially want in her head. I've also discovered, to my great surprise, that I have a favorite Sheryl Crow song. It's the one with the poncho and "pray for mosquitoes."

"Hello, ladies and gentlemen," says the Troll today, momentarily blowing our minds. "Do you know what you'd like?"

We notice that the high-ponytail waitress isn't working. In her place is a young Mexican or Central American woman with a shy smile. We ask after high-ponytail.

"She, uh, ain't working here no more."

While we wait for our food, we confer in whispers. Suzy thinks the Troll has been promoted and is feeling her oats.

"They've created a monster," warns Bob.

"A monstrous lobster, a slobster, a sob sister," murmurs Odin.

On the way back to work, Suzy says, "Someone's got to take the Troll down a peg or two. Maybe sneak up behind her with a sockful of nickels." She stops suddenly and looks up, stricken. "I can't believe I just said that."

As November turns into December, the Bee turns to all-Christmas programming. We stick to our guns through "Rocking around the Christmas Tree," through the Boss's live version of "Santa Claus Is Coming to Town," through every conceivable treatment of "Little Drummer Boy." The row house gets colder, our backs get stiffer, and our lunch hours expand. I've been finding the sudokus increasingly difficult. Eventually, I give up and turn to the Daily Jumble.

Today at Pinky's we stare at our menus for what seems like an eternity. The Troll stands over us, looking impatient in her blankly surprised way. She is wearing a sweatshirt that says, "Stroll For Epilepsy." Finally, we all order Rock Hudsons and she goes away.

"Listen," says Suzy.

Sim-ply ha-ving awon-derfulchrist-mastime . . .

It's the same Paul McCartney song that was playing less than an hour ago on the Eazy 101 radio.

"But wait. Did you notice what the last song was?"

"'Silver Bells,' Mariah Carey."

"Gloria Estefan, actually. Just like on the Bee. What are the odds of that?"

"Are you sure it wasn't Mariah Carey?"

Suzy shakes her head. "It was Gloria Estefan," she says with joyless certainty.

And then John Cougar Mellencamp, "I Saw Mommy Kissing Santa Claus," and then Andy Williams, "Winter Wonderland," which (Suzy insists) is the exact set they played on the Bee. Does Pinky's have the Bee on some sort of tape delay? Suzy asks the Troll what station they're listening to.

"Uh, it's just a station," she says. Suzy looks suspicious.

"Mannheim fucking Steamroller," says Odin. "Nickel socks."

"We must have heard him wrong," I tell Suzy after lunch. But she's shaken.

The Troll is ascendant, the tape-delay mystery continues, and day after day, Odin sits piled up on his chair like a human antenna, like a transmission tower.

"Julie Andrews. Lena Horne. A cup a cup a cup a cup a cup."

Today I can't seem to warm up. I avoid using the bathroom for as long as possible. Why is it so cold back there?

" . . . rememberememberemember . . . "

Also, I can make no sense of the Daily Jumble. In the cartoon clue, a man lies on a psychiatrist's couch and the doctor says, "You have to make this choice. Do you _ _ _ _ _ _ _ _ ?"

I decide I'm coming down with something and take the afternoon off.

The rest of the week is a fever dream. When I return to the row house on Monday, Suzy has given up on the Bee until after Christmas and Bob has rejoined her in the front room. They've doubled up the window plastic, but still the space heater struggles to break 40 degrees.

We throw in the towel—it's not even 11:30—and stagger over to Pinky's, where the tail end of the breakfast crowd is lingering over their eggs. The air feels tropical. The cook sits at the newspaper table, smoking, bathed in radiant light. In here, Christmas—the Bee?—still wafts through the air.

. . . *putting up reindeer, singing songs of joy and peace* . . .

I don't see the Troll.

"Oh, I can't believe we forgot to tell you," says Suzy. "Last Thursday, Bob heard her being yelled at in the back—just getting completely reamed. She must have gotten too big for her britches. Anyway, she was gone on Friday. We think she got fired!"

I'm unprepared for it. I actually feel a lump in my throat as the shyly smiling Mexican or Central American waitress appears, ready to take our orders. The front door opens and in walks Odin. He comes to a stop at the next table, turns toward me, unwraps his face. His commanding eye locks down on mine. He says, to me, unmistakably,

"Cry me a river to skate away on."

And they come, tears.

KITTY AND ISAAC STORIES

Safe, Reliable, Courteous

Kitty falls into a deep, instant sleep outside San Bernardino as the bus labors up the Cajon Pass. The whine of the engine invades her dreams. She's trapped in the cargo hold of an airplane. She's engulfed in a swarm of insects. She's crawling on hands and knees through an air-conditioned tunnel.

When she fights her way back to consciousness, she finds herself wedged into a fetal position with her head jammed into the carpet-covered wall. It's still dark out, and the bus is idling somewhere. She sits up and looks out the window. They're in a concrete bay outside a depot. A line of people waits under the fluorescent lights: a young woman holding a sleepy child in pajamas; two box-shaped Mexican men wearing brightly colored knit shirts, their pants sharply creased; and, towering over all of them, a skinny white kid with a nylon gym bag. He looks about Kitty's age, or maybe a few years younger — eighteen or nineteen. He has frizzy, shoulder-length hair. He wears paratrooper pants tucked into engineer boots, and a leather jacket that is much too small for him, exposing several inches above his wrists. The door sighs open and the line shuffles forward. Kitty lies back down and pretends to be asleep, and by the time they reach the interstate she's drifted off.

When she wakes again, the bus is flooded with light. They are traveling across a high plain. Her neck hurts, and she's very thirsty, having forgotten to bring anything to drink. She takes a fat paperback out of her backpack: *The Executioner's Song*. On the cover is a flat western landscape at sunset. A silhouette of power lines vanishes into darkness. Kitty plans to lose herself in the book while they cross the vast interior of the continent, but now she's distracted by the glare outside her window. She traces an overpass to a distant town and tries to imagine living in one of the white ranch houses, a mile or so beyond the highway. After a while her eyes go out of focus. She falls asleep again.

An angry voice from somewhere in the back of the bus jolts Kitty awake:

"Fuck off, you fucking zombie!"

Another voice, raised to keep up with the first:

"Now that's a shame. Truly a shame, because the Lord wants you to join him—"

"Leave me alone!"

A boy stands up on the seat in front of her to look. The boy's mother pulls him down, but she's staring too.

"He wants you with him in the kingdom of heaven. All will be forgiven—"

"I didn't do anything, genius, so why do I need to be forgiven?"

Heads are craned all the way down the aisle, but Kitty doesn't need to turn around. She knows, from a sullen note in the first voice, that it's the skinny white guy she'd seen getting on the bus last night. The voices get louder until, finally, the driver pulls onto the shoulder and comes up the aisle, leaning his bulk on every other seat. He looks more bored than irritated.

"If you gentlemen can't keep it down, you're both getting put off this bus in Flagstaff. You hear me?"

"I didn't do anything," the sullen voice protests. "This clown won't shut up."

"Okay, you, come with me."

The driver puts the skinny kid in the seat next to Kitty and lumbers back up the aisle.

"I fucking hate Christians," her new seatmate says as the bus merges into the traveling lane. He takes a sketchpad and a pencil out of his gym bag and begins drawing. When the little boy pops up over the seat again, staring at him with frank interest, he says, "Take a picture. It'll last longer." The boy's mother yanks him down. Kitty can see him peering out between the seats. "Kids like me because I'm weird-looking," her seatmate says. He goes back to his drawing—some kind futuristic car. He works quickly and expertly, shading with the side of his pencil lead.

The boy stands on his seat again. "Can you draw me something?" he asks. This time his mother leaves him alone.

"Yeah, okay. Do you like dune buggies?"

"I don't know," he says shyly.

Kitty's seatmate draws a dune buggy. And then, on command, a dog and a truck. "Now I'm gonna make something scary," he says. He draws a skeleton. After considering it for a minute, pencil to lips, he adds a pirate's hat and a sword, dripping with blood. He tears the sheet off and hands it to the little boy.

"You know what's scary?" the boy says. "A bat!"

"Skeletons are scarier than bats," he says with authority.

"No, bats are scarier."

Kitty's seatmate snorts. "You're nuts." He puts his drawing pad away.

"Bats bats bats!" sings the boy, and his mother yanks him down again.

In Flagstaff everyone gets off the bus to stretch their legs. Kitty buys some cheese crackers and a soda from the vending machines in the station. Back outside, she finds her seatmate smoking a cigarette. He offers her one, but she shakes her head.

"How far are you going?" she asks.

He's going to his father's house in South Jersey, a town called Cherry Hill.

"I've heard of that. What's it like?"

"Cheery Hell," he says by way of comment.

Actually, she thinks, he's not weird looking at all. He has classically handsome features: a long, straight nose and hazel eyes, a Dudley Do-Right dimple in his strong chin. There's motility to his face, though; it changes with each new thought. That must be why kids stare at him.

"I'm Kitty," she says.

"Isaac." He crushes his cigarette under his boot.

Ten minutes later they're in their seats waiting for the stragglers to board. A young man in a dark suit gives Isaac a baleful look as he passes. He has short hair, and his face is pink with razor rash and acne.

"Have you heard the good news about Satan?" Isaac asks him in a chipper voice.

Kitty sees a sign for the Petrified Forest an hour outside of Flagstaff, but there's no evidence of it in the landscape. She thought Arizona would look like a Krazy Kat cartoon: buttes and mesas etched with deep orange and blue shadows, undistorted in the dry air, so that they would seem unnaturally close, as if they were passing in slow motion just outside her window and she could reach over and brush them with her hand.

Though the actual scenery is boring—flat and grey, with rubbly hills in the far distance—she doesn't look away until the sun has crossed the sky. Isaac has been, by turns, napping and drawing. He's working on another futuristic car now. When he notices Kitty looking, he positions his sketchbook to give her a better view.

"That's really good," she says. "It looks like a real industrial drawing."

"I can draw anything." It's not a boast, just a statement of fact. "I was supposed to go to the Art Center in Pasadena. It's the ultimate school for auto design."

"What happened?"

"I don't know. Why bother?"

"I guess so you can design cars?"

"That's true," he says, as though it hadn't occurred to him. She pulls out her book.

"I read that," Isaac says. "Gary Gilmore. He kicks ass."

Kitty has no patience for serial-killer worship. It reminds her of high school boys in Charles Manson shirts.

"A kid offered me ten thousand dollars to kill his brother," he says. "But I was too much of a pussy."

She lets it pass. Opens her book and begins, at last, to read.

They have a half hour in Gallup to get something to eat. Kitty walks outside the station, hoping to find a store of some kind. She looks up and down the wide street and sees nothing but motels and gas stations, so she gets a cheeseburger at the Burger King in the station and eats it leaning against the wall outside. When she gets on the bus, Isaac's seat is empty. She climbs over his gym bag and buries her nose in *The Executioner's Song* until the motion of the bus breaks her concentration. She scrambles back over his bag and up the aisle yelling "Wait! Wait!" and the bus comes to a stop again.

The driver is irritated this time. "You got three minutes to get him, Miss, or I'm leaving the both of you here."

She finds Isaac inside the station, staring at a rack of car magazines.

Kitty's eyes follow the power lines, bobbing rhythmically against the dimming sky. The ground beneath recedes into shadows. After a while it's too dark to see anything. She doesn't feel like reading, so she turns to Isaac and asks, "Did someone really try to get you to kill his brother?"

"Yeah."

"Why?"

"Because his brother was an evil thug, that's why. It's a long story. You want to hear it?"

"Sure." She leans back in her seat.

"So, this kid, right, he was a friend of this guy I was hanging around with. His parents died in a car accident and left everything, the house and everything, to him and his brother. But his brother wouldn't give him any money. Wouldn't even let him stay in the house. Made him sleep on a lawn chair in the fucking garage and beat on him whenever he tried to get inside. So this kid decided the only way to get the money was if someone killed his brother. He was looking for a stranger, someone who couldn't be linked to the crime, and, but, also, he, the kid, would be at work and have an alibi. That was his concept. He saw it in a movie—he had a portable TV in the garage. One of those little things with a six inch screen and a handle. It was fucking pathetic. But like I said, I was too much of a pussy."

Kitty thinks of the phrase *scary drifter*, but it doesn't seem to fit Isaac—maybe because he's so chatty. "Where was this?" she asks.

"El Cajon. Have you ever been to El Cajon? It's totally beat."

"Is that where you got on?" she asks, but she knows that can't be right. It was a big bus depot.

"No, that was Phoenix."

Kitty wants to keep him talking. "What were you doing in El Cajon?" she asks, and Isaac tells his story.

He graduated from high school last spring, in Cherry Hill, but instead of going to the car design school in Pasadena he drove to Phoenix, which is where his mother lives, in a VW bus that he'd fixed up at the garage where he worked after school. His mother said she could get him a job, but when he got there it turned out the job she had in mind was packing crates in a tile factory for three dollars an hour less than what he was making at the garage. On top of that, he got kicked out of his mother's house after only two weeks.

"Why did she throw you out?"

"Who knows? Her mongoloid boyfriend probably wanted me out so he could fuck her on the couch."

So he took a room in a wino hotel. Then he saw an ad in the back of the paper: the National Park Service was hiring seasonal workers. He went out to Sequoia and got a job washing dishes at a big lodge. He had a room in the dormitory, but his room-mate got them both thrown out for selling acid. After that, they drove the VW to San Francisco and parked it in the Haight and slept in Isaac's bus. They met some "really nice fags" who fed them and let them take showers and didn't even hit on them or anything. But then Isaac's friend got picked up for shoplifting a hairdryer from Woolworth.

"A *hairdryer*?"

"Yeah." Isaac snorted. "He was really into his hair."

The cops told them they'd be arrested for vagrancy if they saw Isaac's VW in the Haight again. Isaac's friend was from El Cajon, and he said they could probably get jobs there. But El Cajon was totally beat. There was nothing to do there but kill that other guy's brother, and Isaac was too much of a pussy. So he drove back to Phoenix because he couldn't think of what else to do. He got a job washing dishes at a Denny's and moved back into the wino hotel. But then his VW bus shit the bed, and he got disgusted with the whole situation and called his old boss at the garage in New Jersey, who wired him money for a bus ticket.

"I don't think my dad's gonna let me move back in, though. He's still pissed off about the Art Center. I'll figure something out when I get there."

They have an hour and a half layover in Albuquerque. Outside the depot, Kitty feels the October cold for the first time and wishes she had a warm coat. It's only nine p.m., but nothing seems to be open. She walks through an empty plaza. Frail saplings in concrete tree-wells suggest a recent campaign of civic revitalization—apparently unsuccessful. The only street life is gathered on the sidewalk outside a 7-Eleven. Kitty stocks up: a loaf of squishy rye bread, a squeeze jar of yellow mustard, a pack of bologna, two bottles of club soda. When she boards the bus again she's relieved to see Isaac already in his seat. He offers her a chocolate donut from a box at his feet.

"Look what else I got," he says, opening a black plastic case. Tucked into the foam lining is a laser pointer and a set of interchangeable tips. He takes the pointer out, clicks it on and off, waggles it back and forth. He changes the tip. Now, instead of a dot of light, a little red smiley face zips across the seats in front of them.

"I hope you didn't waste too much money on that," Kitty says.

"I love this kind of executive crap."

They eat bologna sandwiches. They talk and Isaac draws, until Kitty notices that the bus has gone dark around them. Everyone else is quiet. When they reach up to turn out their lights, she feels a pro forma flutter, a possibility of sexual contact, but nothing happens. Isaac reclines his seat all the way back. Kitty balls up her extra sweater into a pillow and leans against the window. She rests her eyes on the shapes of the hills, a shade blacker than the sky.

She sleeps. She sleeps through Tucumcari. The lights of the Amarillo depot wake her, but Isaac sleeps on, turned toward her in his seat with his mouth hanging open.

They transfer to a different bus in Oklahoma City. They're traveling together now. They've figured out that their routes won't diverge until Harrisburg, Pennsylvania, where she'll head north and he'll keep going east. It occurs to Kitty that the passengers on this bus can't tell that they didn't know each other thirty-six hours earlier. Isaac makes friends with a little boy a few years older than the "bats bats bats" kid. He lets the boy play with the laser pointer. They collaborate on a comic strip, passing the drawing pad back and forth across the aisle. Their comic is about a giant crab monster.

"You have to make one claw bigger," Isaac says. "Crabs have one big claw and one smaller one, because they're left-handed or right-handed, like people. Did you ever see a crab swim? I did. They swim upside-down in the water with their claws pointed down. They paddle around with those little back feet."

Kitty listens while he tries to explain black holes to the boy, and the Trail of Tears, and carburetors vs. fuel injectors. When the boy and his mother get off in Joplin, Missouri, Isaac puts his pad away and looks out the window with Kitty. He points out an abandoned gas station covered with spidery vines on the two-lane road alongside the interstate.

"That's Route 66," says the man who has taken the seat across the aisle. He has a steel-grey flattop and wears work pants and a hunting jacket. "We'll follow it all the way to St. Louis. Then it doglegs north, on up to Chicago."

"Get out," said Isaac, "That's Route 66?"

"Sure it is. Like the song. *If you're planning da-da-da motor west, take the highway that's the highway that's the best . . .*"

Kitty watches the roadside with new interest while Isaac falls into conversation with their neighbor. He tells Isaac about a long-ago road trip he took with his first wife, in a red Toronado with a white landau top. As the man talks about the places he and his wife stopped, Kitty realizes that they've been shadowing Route 66 since Flagstaff.

The bus station in St. Louis, where they have an hour-long layover, is a shock after the cinderblock bunkers and temporary sheds they've seen in the last couple of days. It has a high, vaulted ceiling supported by ornate columns. Isaac guesses it's a decommissioned bank. They walk around with their heads craned, looking at the art deco clocks and milk-glass chandeliers. On the ground level, though, all is bus station squalor. A sawhorse blocks the entrance to the men's room. A bum inventories an overflowing trashcan next to the shuttered newsstand. The candy machine has been emptied of everything but gum. Kitty is content to refill her club soda bottle at the drinking fountain and snack on some peanut butter and bread they got earlier that day in Springfield, Missouri, but Isaac needs cigarettes. She gets back on the bus and reads her book while he goes out looking for a convenience store. She knows about Gary Gilmore, so she knows where the story goes. The book runs on inevitability rather than suspense—from frustration, greed, loneliness to murder, trial, firing squad. She finds it almost unbearable, but she's gotten sucked in anyhow. She wants to reach back there and knock Gilmore off the path he's on.

Where, she wonders, is Isaac? Finally, he gets on the bus and sits down. He stares at the seat in front of him. Kitty asks if he found a store, and he grunts in response. It's obvious that something has happened, but she doesn't know him well enough to coax it out of him. They're silent as the bus crosses the Mississippi, past East St. Louis, into the moonless Illinois night. Kitty sees a road marker for Historical Route 66. She thinks of pointing it out, but Isaac is still staring at the seat back, so she says nothing.

After a while they turn east on Interstate 70, leaving Route 66 behind. The bus stops in Effingham for a twenty minute break. Kitty, grasping for conversation, asks Isaac if he's going outside to smoke.

"No, I am not going outside to smoke, because I don't have any *smokes*," he says.

"You didn't get cigarettes in St. Louis?"

Finally it comes out. Before he even got two blocks from the station in St. Louis, Isaac was mugged for his wallet and all the money he had left after he bought his bus ticket.

"Oh my God, Isaac. Did he have a gun?"

"He had something under his sweatshirt. Maybe it was just his hand, I don't know."

"Why didn't you say anything?"

"What am I supposed to say? I'm a big pussy?"

"What are you gonna do? Can you call someone?" Kitty asks, and then realizes Isaac hasn't made any plans beyond getting off the bus in Cherry Hill or wherever he's getting off the bus. She isn't sure anyone in his family even knows he's on his way home. "Can you call your father?"

He doesn't answer.

"Your mother?"

He snorts.

"Well, don't worry. I have enough money for both of us," she says, and she understands now that they are not parting ways in Harrisburg. Isaac will come with her, or she will go with him, and she'll make him see that nothing is inevitable.

Garbage Head

Isaac went north on 42nd Street, conscious of walking through tangible air. Out of the shower for fifteen minutes and already his clothes were stuck to him. Coppery light vibrated on every reflective surface. The heat that muffled all other sounds somehow amplified the hum of insects in the drooping boughs of the old maples. Hummm, hummm. He heard a mocking reference in the call and response. Isaac this, Isaac that, the insects said.

He'd been on a floor-sanding crew for a few months, saving up money for his own wheels. He'd managed to put aside three hundred fifty dollars toward a red Aerostar he had his eye on, but his days were a hamster wheel: go to work, pick up a stromboli on the way home, eat half of the stromboli for supper, eat the other half for breakfast, go to work again. Today was Saturday, though—payday—so he forced himself out the door and headed up to the Snakehouse to see Poison Idea and get drunk. He had a right.

The sun had dropped below the onion domes and dunce caps of Victorian West Philly. He crossed Walnut Street, leaving behind long blocks of front porches and window grates and entering a zone of drive-by commerce. 7-Eleven, Pep Boys. The aroma of kung pao chicken hung in the wet air. From 38th and Lancaster he could see that there was already a small crowd outside the Snakehouse. He veered diagonally across Lancaster to the liquor store and bought himself a forty, slipping the last wilted bill in his wallet through the little plastic window. He patted the untouched wad of payday twenties in his front pocket, just to be sure, and squared his shoulders to face the people.

Of course the first person he saw was Kitty's friend Lisa, sitting on the curb. Seeing her put him in danger of thinking about Kitty, which, if he wanted to do that he would have picked up a stromboli and stayed home. To make matters worse, Lisa was talking to a beautiful, creamy-skinned girl— Linda? Leena? Lola?—one of those witchypoo girls he always saw around West Philly barefoot, in velvet elf dresses, smelling like hippie candles. He didn't want to risk making eye contact with either of them, so he ducked into the vacant lot next to the liquor store.

Isaac sat down on a truck tire and straightened out his legs. His knees ached from squatting with the edging sander. He drank his forty as fast as he could, in gulps that outpaced the garbagey taste of the malt liquor, and waited for full darkness. While he waited, he thought about the Aerostar. It had AC. Also plush velour seats and power windows. He'd seen it parked at the gas station on Baltimore Ave with a for-sale sign in the back window and talked to the mechanic who was selling it. He was pretty sure he could get it for less than the nine hundred the guy was asking. He let himself imagine loading tools in the back: his own sander and edger, a chop saw and a top-nailer, a good compressor. Sam, his boss, had a full-size van. The way Isaac figured, a minivan was the ideal work truck: comfortable, civilized, easy on the gas. Take out the bench seats and you could fit a sheet of plywood in the back. Best of all, minivans were despised by your average goon and therefore stealth. He'd been telling people about minivans forever. No one listened to him. After a while he heard the first band start up inside. He stopped off for another forty and crossed the street. Lisa and the witchypoo girl were gone, thank God.

The Snakehouse was actually a compound of two connected buildings. To get to the warehouse where the bands played, you passed through a storefront gallery. People were lined up against the back wall, faces in shadow, sweat-glazed arms and legs lit in flashes by the streetlight coming through the big front windows. An industrial floor fan moved the air around. Isaac forked over his dollars and got his hand stamped and plunged into the sweltering cave next door.

The warehouse was still nearly empty—just a few guys holding paper bags, standing around at the far end of the room. On the low plywood stage, a skinny kid lunged in tight circles, croaking satanically into a mic he held in a white-knuckle grip. The sound coming out of him seemed to have nothing to do with his body. He reminded Isaac of a ventriloquist's dummy. Again and again, he narrowly avoided colliding with a contrastingly large and immobile kid grinding away at a guitar that hung almost to his knees. His face was hidden behind a curtain of hair. These guys were okay. The logo on the kick drum was amateurish: the letters "G.F.A," snared in a spider web. Isaac could definitely help them out there.

The back door was propped open, and when Isaac's eyes adjusted he saw a silhouette in the doorway and recognized the cones of Bozo the Clown hair. It was Greg—Craig? Shit, he was terrible with names. A Snakehouse regular. He and whoever he was talking to were huddling in a furtive way that set off Isaac's drug radar.

"Hey, Greg!" He yelled to be heard over the satanic croaking as he approached the drug huddle. "Gimme some of that! What is it?"

Greg and his friend exchanged a look and Greg leaned in close to Isaac's ear. "NNDM," he yelled.

"What?"

"MNDN."

"*What* is it?"

"NNDN."

"Whatever. Gimme it."

The three went back out to Lancaster Ave and around the corner to Greg's friend's car. The guy started explaining about the MNMN. He said it was a compound he and his partner had just invented. They were Penn students or chemists or something. It was cool, actually, what he was saying. If you came up with a new molecule that the government didn't know about, it wasn't technically illegal.

"What do you do, snort it?"

A few minutes later, Isaac was back in the cave watching the first band break down their equipment. He didn't feel much of anything. Maybe a little jittery. It had, if possible, gotten hotter in the warehouse, so he stepped out the back door to wait it out between sets. Behind the buildings that made up the Snakehouse, the storefront gallery and the warehouse, were the ruins of another warehouse. Gutted by fire and exposed to the elements, it had grown over with city flora. It was like a courtyard. Isaac leaned against the remnants of a brick wall and breathed in the sour perfume of the ghetto palms. Kitty called them "trees of heaven."

This was his favorite part of the Snakehouse complex. If he could get over his shyness and penetrate the scene, he'd transform this place. He would make thrones out of the rubble, and an amphitheater of scary organic shapes like Gaudí. He would paint the back wall white and project movies, and he would be the king of it out here. He wondered if Lisa had seen him, or if she'd said anything about him to the other Snakehouse people. He thought now that she *had* seen him. He was sure she'd looked at him without *looking* at him.

Maybe he hadn't done enough of that MMMM. He took out the bindle and snorted half of what was left. There was a warm, spreading sensation, like right after you piss your pants, but he felt it all over his body. It was interesting, but it only lasted for a minute, so he snorted the rest and sank into the deep shadow of the warehouse.

A slow, kicking beat pulled him back to the surface, and then a single bass note in the key of dirge. And then a guitar riff that traveled like a slow, sludgy current on wire, twisting into the shapes of letters. HDR? FDR? D.R.I., G.F.A., MMND, MDM. He followed the sound back into the cave, which was filled now with smoke and fleshy flesh and sulphurous light. It was hotter than ever. He felt a splash on his neck. Looking up, he became transfixed by the condensation pooling on the pipe above him until, suddenly and irrevocably, it occurred to him that he might have puked all over himself. He tried to get closer to the light coming from the stage so he could see if it was true. He searched for an opening in the wall of meat, then gave up and fought his way back in the other direction and through the door to the gallery, gulping for air as he burst out onto Lancaster Ave, but finding only warm gel. There was no puke on him.

He went back across the street to the vacant lot and sat on his truck tire and stared at the throbbing halo around the streetlight. The climate on Lancaster Ave had achieved a reptilian kind of homeostasis with the climate in his skull. After a while, he realized that the music had stopped. He got up, too quickly, and his stomach heaved. A flume of malt liquor splattered the weeds and the tire and the brick wall. He stood for a while, bent over, feeling suddenly clammy, and when he looked up, the halo around the streetlight had disappeared. Whatever that shit was that he'd snorted, it seemed to be out of his system. What a rip-off. He decided to get another forty and walk home.

A bum stood in front of the liquor store. Hot as it was, he was wearing a colorless windbreaker, zipped all the way up to his chin. He looked familiar. Something about the way he was hopping from foot to foot. His thin ankles poked out of orthopedic-looking shoes.

Of course, it was Eddie. Isaac hadn't recognized him at first, because he knew him from the deli on Chester, near his house. Eddie was like part of the street furniture, as fixed to his spot as a mailbox or a streetlight. Once, he'd shown Eddie his sketchbook, and ever since, the guy acted like he was in love with him or something.

"Hello, Picasso!" Eddie's face opened up into a gummy smile when he saw Isaac.

It occurred to Isaac that he'd been followed. "What are you doing here, Eddie?" he said.

"What am I doing here? This my old stomping grounds. What are *you* doing here, blessed boy?"

"Right now I'm going to buy myself some beer." Eddie kept on moistly beaming at him. "Aw hell, you want a forty? My treat, buddy. I just got paid."

"You don't have to give me nothing. I ain't ask you for nothing," said Eddie.

"I know," said Isaac, "I want to."

He went inside and asked for two Olde Englishes.

"You gotta take it someplace else though," said the cashier.

Isaac reached in his front pocket. Instead of the roll of twenties, he pulled out a wad of Kleenex.

"Fuck."

He tried his other pockets, and then his wallet. No, his roll was gone. "Forget it," he said. He walked out, past Eddie, and west on Lancaster.

"Hey! Picasso!" Eddie called after him.

"Sorry, Eddie," Isaac yelled without turning around.

Six fucking days on his knees, scraping and edging and sucking in polyurethane fumes. Apparently he'd done all that for free, like the fucking slave that he was. His stomach heaved again, but there was nothing in it. Yuppie bitch telling Sam to "make sure those guys don't go in my kitchen." Drinking out of the fucking hose like a dog. With what he'd had in his pocket he could have paid for the Aerostar.

Six days. Fuck. He thought of the Penn guy, the chemist. Maybe he'd dropped his roll in the car. Then he thought about the other guy, his roommate's friend, lying on the couch in front of the TV when he came home and got in the shower. Of course. That piece of shit went through his pockets. Isaac was sure of it.

He turned on 42nd Street, across Walnut and into the green canopy of the old maples. The air was still heavy, but the insects had gone quiet. When he stopped to listen for them, he heard footsteps and spun around. Eddie was following him, half a block behind.

"I'm sorry, Eddie. I lost my money."

"I told you I ain't ask for nothing. I'm headed home just like you are."

"Okay." He waited while Eddie caught up and they walked together silently.

"I lost my whole paycheck," Isaac said after a bit. "In cash. A roll of twenties."

"I'm sorry."

"Yeah, it blows. I know who took it, too."

"You gonna get it back?"

"I don't know. Probably not. I don't want to talk about it. So, that's your old stomping grounds? Over there by Lancaster Ave?"

"Ludlow. 37th and Ludlow."

"Isn't that all Penn buildings? I never noticed any houses over there."

"It used to be nothing *but* houses over there, before they plowed it all under. Yeah, that's where I grew up, 37th and Ludlow."

"No shit? Your house got knocked down?"

"Not just *my* house," Eddie said, hopping a little. "We had a— a—" He waggled his hands. "Over on 34th and Walnut we had a movie theater, stores, everything you might need right there in the neighborhood. A drug store. I used to run deliveries after school, take my money and go to the movies."

"I never heard about that."

"I expect you haven't," he said. "I am not one bit surprised. I call that place Atlantis now. Atlantis, you know? But the real name we called it was Black Bottom."

Kitty would have wanted to know about that, thought Isaac a little sadly. It was the kind of thing they'd talked about: secret history.

"Penn tore it down so they could build all those labs and shit?"

"Well, that's one thing. The other thing is, they ain't want us in a so-called slum. So now everybody living in a worse slum somewhere else, if they living anywhere at all.

"Wait, did Penn tear it down or the city?"

"You tell me the difference."

Isaac wasn't sure what that meant, but it sounded right. "How old are you, Eddie?" he asked.

Eddie stopped for a moment, and Isaac waited while he thought about it. "I'm forty-two years old. Forty-two, or forty-one or forty-three. One of them."

When they got to his house, Isaac said good night to Eddie and let himself in.

Eddie crossed Chester Street and looked up to the attic window, where the blessed boy stayed. A light went on. Pearls before swine, Eddie thought. When the light went out again he turned to leave and noticed something under the tire of a car. He squatted down to look. Yes, there it was. A roll of twenty-dollar bills.

The Minivan

I met Isaac when he was doing some work at my house. I think he asked me out because he admired my fiberglass spaghetti lamp. He was foxy, punk rock, bratty in his banana curls and calculator watch. Mostly, he was hilarious. On our first date, at a bar in South Philly, he told me all about his plan to poison the crackheads in his neighborhood by scattering cyanide-filled vials on the sidewalk, and about shooting pigeons by the bucketful in a warehouse he'd once lived in. He had me in stitches with his megalomaniacal fantasies of turning a certain abandoned factory into a fortress of solitude, where he would build his own personal road-warrior batmobile. We sat at the padded vinyl bar and hoisted mug after mug of lager, thrilled to have found one another. Outside, we groped behind a dumpster. We groped *in* a dumpster. Of course, this was before I knew he wasn't kidding about any of it.

One morning a few weeks into our affair, we sat on his sofa and looked at his photo album. Here was baby Isaac, standing unsteadily in a hallway, gripping a bench for support. Here was Isaac as a slack-lipped high school metalhead, eyes stoned and affectless beneath a frizzy mullet. Here he was perched high up on a roof truss in the warehouse, aiming a BB gun at the camera. Next to him was his old dog, Death Isaac, since lost in an acrimonious break-up. There were random snapshots of things he liked: a brutalist municipal building, an ornate Victorian window grate, a boat in a weed-choked lot behind a cyclone fence, christened "The A-HOLE" in stick-on mailbox letters. We flipped through pages and pages of photos of floors he'd installed or refinished over the years. Isaac described each one: red pine, tongue-and-groove oak, maple parquet. Occasionally there was someone in the background or off to one side holding a shop vac or a bucket, but Isaac didn't identify them as he leafed through the album with me.

He stopped at a picture of a skinny blonde girl in the passenger seat of a van. I thought he was going to tell me about an ex-girlfriend; maybe the one who'd kept Death Isaac. Instead, he began waxing nostalgic about the van she was sitting in. It was an Aerostar, he said, with plush velour seats and AC and power everything, and it was the nicest car he'd ever had. This launched a disquisition on the subject of minivans, which he said were perfect work vehicles. A minivan got better gas mileage than a pickup truck or a full-sized van, but you could still fit a 4 x 8 sheet of plywood in the back. And then you could sit up front in a nice civilized captain's chair, with a cup-holder and everything. He liked his creature comforts. He told me he had drawn plans for a prototype of a modern minivan when he was ten years old, and he therefore felt that it was, in a certain way, his invention.

But Isaac had no minivan now, and indeed no driver's license. An epileptic, he had crashed his Aerostar into the side of a church during a grand mal seizure. The Aerostar was totaled and he was taken to the emergency room, where the doctor who treated him put a medical suspension on his driver's license. He couldn't get his license restored until he could prove he hadn't had a seizure for six months. This would require appointments with neurologists. Also blood tests, various costly scans and imagings, and who knew what else. Furthermore, he wasn't remotely seizure-free. He had hangover seizures, stress-related seizures, strobe light/trance music/op art seizures. He had just-for-the-hell-of-it seizures. "Everyone should have a seizure," he told me. "It's intense." He hadn't seen a neurologist since they sprang him from the hospital. He couldn't. He had no health insurance. And rather than apply for Medicaid, he'd done what came naturally: he had slid effortlessly, numbly, fatalistically off the grid.

Somehow, he was maintaining a floor-sanding business on his bicycle. A floor sander, in case you've never seen one, is a huge, unwieldy thing made out of cast metal. Isaac's weighed probably two hundred pounds. Then there was the buffer, the edger, milk crates full of sandpaper, five gallon buckets of polyurethane—all this had to be transported to and from the job. Astonishingly, he was able to get the housewives who engaged his services to shuttle him and all his equipment and supplies in their SUVs and drive him to Home Depot and Diamond Tool and Bell Flooring, often making several trips a day due to his chronic disorganization. He wasn't apologetic or even particularly nice about it—he was basically a petulant, sarcastic teenager about it—and yet these housewives loved him with all the exasperation and indulgence that their inner soccer moms possessed. I saw it with my own eyes. They clucked disapprovingly at his diatribes against recycling and in favor of apocalyptic forms of population control, but still they made him nice lunches and sewed buttons on his shirts and paid him in cash because he didn't have a bank account.

His inscrutable charm worked on me, too. The clichés pile up as I try to explain: He made me laugh. I could be myself around him. I'd never met anyone like him, gimlet-eyed and crazy in equal measure. Ultimately, what really got to me was that he was so guileless. He concealed none of his emotions, positive or negative; everything he felt seemed to register on the surface of his skin. Within a month he had moved into my house.

Summer came. Isaac and I rode our bikes all over town, and he took me to his favorite spots in his old neighborhood. He showed me buildings he'd pillaged or planned to pillage for glass wall sconces, doorknobs, and other treasures. At a decommissioned bank under the Frankford El he had me look through a hole in the plywood at a grand chandelier hanging from the vaulted ceiling. In the vacant lots around his old house, junkies had arranged sofas and chairs, milk crates, and industrial spools into cozy conversation pits.

At some point in our travels we came across a mid-'80s Dodge Caravan, sun-dulled and putty-colored, beached on a Fishtown sidewalk in the shade of an ailanthus tree. It had a for-sale sign in the back window. "I'm gonna buy that minivan," he said, and he wrote the phone number down in his sketchbook. I probably laughed, if I reacted at all.

I forgot all about it. Then one afternoon I came home and found Isaac sitting on our stoop, shit-faced drunk. Having nowhere to be that day, he'd polished off a bottle of vodka he found in the freezer and then called the phone number in his sketchbook. "If you can get it to South Philly, I'll give you four hundred dollars cash for it," he'd told the no-doubt delighted owner of the Caravan. A few minutes after I got home, the minivan pulled up to the curb in a cloud of white smoke and rattled to a stop. I took a look and went back in the house.

After a while, Isaac staggered inside and sat across from me at the kitchen table.

"That's one happy sonofabitch that got your four hundred dollars," I said.

"Yeah? Well, how am I supposed to get the money for anything better? I can't even drive my tools around. Are *you* going to buy me an Aerostar? No? That's what I thought. Everyone has a fucking minivan but me."

I asked all the obvious questions: how was he going to

register it? Was he planning to just drive around without a license? Had he even looked at the engine before he forked over his money? But this was all beside the point. Isaac was sick of not having a minivan, so he'd called the guy, and now he had a minivan. And not only was I not happy for him, I was giving him crap about it. As for his driver's license, as far as he was concerned, he was so thoroughly fucked that there was no point in thinking about that either.

"Fine," I said, "don't call me when you get pulled over for driving around without a license plate."

Isaac let out a long, quarrelsome fart as he contemplated this, then disappeared into the basement and reemerged with a roll of duct tape and some scissors. He grabbed a box of Cheerios off the table, dumped its contents in the sink, and cut a license plate-sized rectangle out of the cardboard. I followed him outside to see what he would do next. He looked up the street, wrote three letters on the piece of cardboard with a sharpie, then looked down the other way and added four numbers. He taped the cardboard onto the Caravan's license plate holder and got in. The engine turned over after several tries, and the minivan lurched to the end of the block and vanished around the corner.

After a few hours of furious paging, I heard from him. He was at his friend Larry's house. It sounded like there was a party going on.

"Hey, what are you doing?" he asked—as though there'd been no fight and no angry paging. "You'll never guess what. You know that Silvertone Dan Electro I told you about? The one I saw at the junk shop at Frankford and York? Larry bought it. The same guitar."

"You drove that piece of shit van to West Philly? Without a plate?"

"I have a plate. I make my *own* plates!"

"Isaac, I'll say it again. You don't have an inspection sticker, insurance, you don't even have a driver's license."

"That stuff's for chumps. Will you stop worrying? I'm telling you, nothing's gonna happen. This is how we roll in Philly. Hey, if I'd had a minivan yesterday, *I* could have bought this Dan Electro. The case has a little amp in it. You just plug it right into the case. It's totally adorable—right up your alley. You should come over here and check it out."

"And you're drunk."

"Aw man, just come over or leave me alone," he said and hung up.

I got on my bike and headed over to Larry's. Did I think I was going to talk Isaac into leaving the minivan there, or did I just feel like I was missing a good party? Who knows. I'd only been with Isaac a few months, and already I was tired of being the heavy.

The ride was calming. I felt the bad mood slipping off as I rode across the Schuylkill, up Spruce, past the food trucks around the Penn campus. I coasted down Woodland Ave, sweetly dappled in the summer twilight. From the depths of Clark Park came the first cool breath of the evening. By the time I got to Larry's, I wasn't angry anymore. Someone handed me a cold bottle of beer. I found Isaac down in the basement, grinding away on Larry's funny little Dan Electro. I drank my beer and threw my bike in the Caravan and we headed home. Isaac leaned his seat back and dangled one arm out the window, his profile bobbing to some inner soundtrack, and I put my feet up on the dashboard and rolled down the window. I let the night air wash over me. This felt good. But the transmission was definitely slipping a little.

Isaac was out in front of the house every day working on the Caravan, and I was often out there keeping him company.

Frank, a mechanic from the garage across the street, took pity on Isaac and let him borrow some tools. I would set up a lawn chair and read magazines while Isaac crawled around under the van. Occasionally I'd be called on to hold down some greasy flange while he listened to the engine, or sit in the van and tell him if a gauge moved or a light went on. He took the transmission out and had it rebuilt, which cost him six hundred and fifty dollars. The brakes were leaking fluid. He replaced the master cylinder, then the wheel cylinders, and finally the brake lines. Most of the exhaust was shot. The tailpipe, it turned out, was hanging by a rusty bracket, unconnected to anything. He was afraid the explosive noise was attracting too much attention, so he replaced the pipe all the way up to the manifold.

I stopped keeping track of how much money Isaac poured into the Caravan. Still, he seemed pleased with it. "Look how tight the steering is," he'd say, giving the wheel a jaunty wiggle.

Sometimes I'd run into Frank and he'd ask, "How's Isaac making out with that minivan?" and then he'd shake his head sadly.

The inevitable happened: Isaac got pulled over making an illegal right on red and the Caravan was impounded. I thought that might be the end of the road, but Isaac was determined to get it back.

We spent the next day in traffic court. When Isaac's name was called, he stood before the judge, a black woman in her fifties with a maroon bob, while an official-looking group conferred around the bench, speaking in a low murmur for several minutes. The bailiff told Isaac to remove his baseball cap and continued to watch him suspiciously as the murmuring at the bench went on. Isaac put his cap back on, and the bailiff told him again to remove it. Finally, the judge addressed him:

"Are you Isaac Baltimore?"

"Yes."

"And is this your car? A . . ." She consulted a sheet of paper in front of her. "A 1983 Dodge Caravan?"

"Can I say something?"

"Is this your car, Mr. Baltimore?"

"I was *born* in this country, and I *work* for a living," he said, giving me a thumbs-up.

The judge ignored this. "Please answer yes or no, Mr. Baltimore. Do you own a 1983 Dodge Caravan?"

"Yes, that's my minivan. Just tell me how much I'm gonna get raped for."

"And do you also own a 1992 Ford LTD?"

"I wish!"

"This . . . this Dodge Caravan is your only vehicle?"

"Yes."

"And is your license plate number MAB1557?"

"Well, I made that up," Isaac said.

"You made it up? I don't understand."

In a tone of nearly exhausted patience, he explained. "I went outside and looked at one plate and wrote down three letters, and then I looked at another plate and wrote down four numbers, and that's how I came up with that number."

There was another conference at the bench and then the judge addressed Isaac again.

"I'm not sure how to handle this," she said. "The license plate number you made up belongs to an individual in Harrisburg, the person who owns this 1992 LTD, which has accumulated $1,840 in parking violations in the City of Harrisburg and another $140 in Reading. You appear to have invented a new kind of violation for which there is no statute."

Isaac straightened a bit and puffed out his chest.

"What are we going to do with you, Mr. Baltimore?"

In the end, it seemed that the city would only release the Caravan to a licensed owner with proof of registration and insurance, and there was nothing the judge could or would do about it. Isaac would not be responsible for the parking tickets, but he would have to pay an $80 impound fee and $260 in fines for driving without a license, registration, or insurance. There would also be a six-month suspension on his driver's license, beginning at such time as his medical suspension had been removed. He was advised to grow up and then dismissed.

It was impossible not to feel sorry for Isaac. For weeks now, he had done nothing but come home from sanding floors all day to work on his minivan, sometimes long after dark. Every dollar he'd earned had gone into it. And now, because he had no health insurance—and with his epilepsy, he was virtually uninsurable—his right to own or drive a car had been revoked indefinitely. I hardly considered myself part of the system; I didn't have health insurance myself, and I hadn't filed a tax return in years; but this, I thought, *this* was what it truly looked like to fall off the grid.

I became obsessed with the idea of restoring Isaac to official personhood. I made appointments at the welfare office and filled out Medicare forms for him so he could see a neurologist and start the process of rebuilding his driving record. I dedicated myself to morale-boosting pep talks, but to him it was pointless. He'd just had another seizure after a boisterous night of drinking with Larry, which meant that, even assuming he saw a neurologist tomorrow, that would only be the beginning of the six seizure-free months he needed to resolve his medical suspension. After that he'd have to wait out the six months he'd racked up for his various legal offenses, which meant it would be a whole year before he could drive the Caravan. Which might as well be ten years. Just thinking about it made him feel like he was going to have a seizure.

Though I knew it was a mistake, I registered the Caravan in my name. Even more stupidly, I let him drive it, and inevitably,

157

he was pulled over for blowing a stoplight. The minivan got impounded again, and his suspension was extended another three months. After that, I started shuttling him and his floor sanding equipment around and taking him to Home Depot, or Bell Flooring, or Diamond Tool. Isaac was becoming a full-time job. And unlike the housewives, I was also on duty weekends, nights and holidays: driving that hideous Caravan around with teeth clenched, hoping no essential engine parts fell off, and thinking wistfully about our bicycle days.

By August we badly needed to get out of town. We were still pretending the Caravan wasn't a disaster, so we decided to drive to Boston to visit my brother. We got a late start on the weekend. I'd filled in as Isaac's helper on a thousand-square-foot buff-and-coat job, and it was well past dark when we headed out. Sometime after midnight, a mile or two east of the Tappan Zee bridge, we had a blowout. I pulled the minivan into a rest area, only to discover that we were traveling without a spare tire. Of course, it had begun to rain. The thought of venturing out into the Westchester County darkness was too awful, and for that matter, useless, so we made a nest on some drop cloths on the back and sank into exhausted sleep.

When I woke up, Isaac was sitting in the wet grass beyond the parking area, staring at the flat tire. He jacked up the back end of the Caravan and took the wheel off, and we walked it back along the highway to the next exit, where we found a gas station at the bottom of the ramp. It was Sunday morning, so of course the garage was closed. We were sitting on a curb, not speaking or looking at each other, when, miraculously, a mid-'80s Dodge Caravan pulled up. It looked exactly like Isaac's—even the same dull putty color—except that it had fake wood-grain paneling. An incongruously well-dressed man got out to pump gas, and Isaac approached him.

It seemed the well-dressed man was on his way to pick up his grandmother and take her to church. After some haggling, he sold us a bald spare for seventy-five dollars. We humped it back up the highway and got going again. Then just outside Newton the engine overheated and blew a radiator hose. We made it to an Auto Zone parking lot and found a payphone and called my brother, who came to pick us up. As soon as we got to his apartment, Isaac started chug-a-lugging beer. He passed out at nine p.m. and had a seizure in his sleep.

After a brief, stupefied visit, we got a ride back to the Auto Zone parking lot. Isaac replaced the radiator hose and we took off down 95. At the Mansfield town line, I noticed the temperature gauge creeping up again, and a mile later it was in the red. I pulled onto the shoulder and we got out. Steam was escaping from under the hood in wisps.

"Ow," Isaac said when he touched the metal.

"Maybe we should let it cool off for a bit."

"I know what I'm doing," he said. He wrapped a shop rag around his hand and lifted the hood. A steaming yellow-green geyser erupted from the radiator, sending us running for cover.

From a safe distance we watched the flume die down. The loud hiss gave way to a series of sharp, surprisingly loud metallic groans and pops.

"Fuck shit fucking fuck fuck *fuck*," Isaac said. "I give up. This cocksucking van has kicked my ass for the last time. Let's just go."

"We can't leave it here, Isaac. They'll trace it back to me."

We hitched into town to get a tow truck. Isaac was quiet all the way back to the garage, where the Caravan was pronounced dead on arrival. The engine had overheated definitively and fatally, cracking the block.

The field around the garage was filled with parts cars. I noticed a familiar-looking grill poking out from the alley between the garage and a rusty trailer next door. I hoped, in vain, that we could get out of there before Isaac saw it.

"Hey," he asked the mechanic, "is that Aerostar running?"

"Sure. Just needs a brake job and a new transmission."

"Can she put it on her credit card?"

"No!" I said, "Isaac, I swear to you that I will do everything in my power to help you get your license back, but I will not register that minivan for you. I can't go through it again."

"But it's not a Caravan," Isaac said. "It's an *Aerostar.*"

"Please don't ask me to do this."

Isaac went dead-eyed. "I figured you wouldn't help me. Why would anyone help me? I'm just some asshole without a car. Fuck me."

Stupid as it seems, we had each drawn a line around the Aerostar. I wouldn't let him use my credit card to buy it, and he wouldn't forgive me. I called my brother to pick us up, but Isaac wouldn't wait. He headed off alone, and a few days later I took a Greyhound back to Philly.

I turned the corner onto my block and saw Isaac in front of the house, loading the last of his things into a Ford Explorer with a Germantown Friends School sticker on the rear window. I ducked back around the corner and waited until the SUV pulled away from the curb. In the house, I found a milk crate on the kitchen table. He'd left three cut-glass doorknob sets, a woodcarving he'd made of a little black dog, and a commemorative Space Shuttle Challenger nightlight. There was also a note:

Dear Kitty, Here is some stuff that you can have. Also

I left you that industrial roller track in the basement, which I can't take because my dad is a freak and he wont let me put anything in his garage. OK I'll see you around I hope.

Thank you Kitty.

Love Isaac.

Mothra

When Isaac got home from work there was a man selling puppies out of a van parked in front of his house. A litter of five, all black, thirty dollars apiece. Isaac leaned into the van to check them out, and one squirmed out of the pile and pushed her snout up the sleeve of his jacket and sighed. He paid the guy and went inside with his new dog, and Kitty found them napping on the couch when she got home an hour later: man and pup sweetly entwined in the evanescing light.

Isaac handed Kitty the puppy. She held it up and saw that it was a girl, with light brown eyes and one ear that stood up and one that fell forward at the tip. The puppy was a surprise but not exactly a shock. Isaac was nothing if not spontaneous. He lived in an eternal now, enjoying instant pleasures and experimenting with impulses. Give him your last few dollars for a quart of milk and he might come back from the store with a car magazine or a novelty keychain instead. He was a person who defrosted the freezer with a plumber's torch. "Don't worry about it," he kept saying, "I know what I'm doing." Sometimes he did and sometimes he didn't, and Kitty wasn't always able to tell the difference before it was too late. She found that she was perpetually on guard against an oncoming disaster. Now, as she cradled the puppy, she told herself that it was Isaac's dog—that they did not *have a dog together*—and she didn't say anything later in the evening when he named the puppy Mothra.

Mothra greeted Kitty at the door when she got home the next day. From the vestibule, she saw Isaac sitting on the kitchen floor with his back to her, tools scattered around him. The floor was strewn with coffee grounds and chewed-up styrofoam. Isaac was absorbed in some job involving a spool of heavy-gauge wire and a red metal box about the size of a pound cake, which he was screwing to the inside of the sink cabinet.

"Man, this dog is sneaky," he said when he noticed Kitty. "Every time I leave her alone she comes in here and gets in the trash." He began unspooling the wire.

"What are you doing?" Kitty asked.

"Mmmm." He twisted the end of the wire around a screw on the side of the box.

"Is that a battery? Wait. Are you putting up a *cattle fence*?"

"Don't worry about it. I know what I'm doing."

"You'll electrocute her!"

Isaac put down the screw gun. This was something that he could not stand: to be interrupted when he had a full head of steam. "I'm not gonna electrocute anyone," he said patiently. "Look, see? It's only two thousand volts—just enough to give her a snootful. It isn't even for cattle. It's for ponies. Or, I don't know, sheep."

It was true that Isaac had a much better grasp of popular science than she did. Still. "No, that can't be how you're supposed to keep a dog out of the trash."

"Look, I know about dogs. How many dogs have you had? That's right, none. And how many dogs have I had? Counting this one, I've had four dogs."

As it happened, Isaac got shocked by the electric fence before Mothra did—several times, in fact—and he decided on his own to take it down.

Kitty had been very interested in animals as a child. She'd read any book she could find about them. Her favorites were *Never Cry Wolf* and *Call of the Wild*. She'd been disturbed, especially in the latter, by the undercurrent of need and violence that seemed to attend stories about people and dogs, and she felt it had put her off the idea of getting a dog herself. Yes, this was Isaac's dog. But after the cattle fence incident, she decided to take some training books out of the library.

"Dogs are pack animals." It was something you heard all the time. The fact that Mothra was destined to form a pack with the people around her meant that the issue of dominance needed to be addressed early on. "Place your puppy gently on its side," one book instructed. "Hold its front paws in one hand and its back paws in the other. Your puppy will not like this, and may even try to bite you." Mothra submitted to the hold patiently. Kitty consulted the illustration to be sure that she was doing it correctly, and seeing that she was, decided to return the books. This was a good puppy.

Isaac took Mothra to the corner for cigarettes, on handyman jobs, for aimless drives; he taught her—or she naturally knew—to run alongside his bike, stopping to wait next to him at corners. But it seemed to Kitty that he treated Mothra too much like a sidekick and not enough like a pet. If he didn't feel like leaving the house, Mothra didn't get a walk. So Kitty started taking her to a churchyard half a mile from the house—an unexpectedly large expanse of grass and trees, hidden from the densely built South Philadelphia neighborhood by a high brick wall.

The church was of some historical significance, part of the national park that included Independence Hall and the Liberty Bell. It was sometimes patrolled by rangers in Smokey the Bear uniforms, but not often enough to keep an unofficial dog park from taking root. From their first visits, Mothra and Kitty began making friends. The churchyard was a village, and the circumstances were socially liberating. Kitty had long conversations with cranks, yuppies, racists, conspiracy theorists, daytime drinkers—all kinds of people she would normally have avoided.

Mothra was especially friendly with a white German Shepherd named Mandy, and because of the relationship between their dogs Kitty was often drawn together with Mandy's owner, Don. He was short, shorter than Kitty, with a grey Afro and mirrored cop glasses. His face was rough-hewn, like a boulder or a chainsaw sculpture, and he had a high, cigarette-shredded voice. Don was a truck driver, out on disability the whole time Kitty knew him, though the details of his injury were mysterious. He had a running prescription for Vicodin, which (he confided to Kitty) he almost always ended up trading in with his dealer for cocaine. He had an unpredictable temper. Some days he would just sit on a tree stump with his back to everyone, other days he was chatty, and either of those moods might disappear in an instant if he felt that Mandy was being in any way aggressed or even snubbed by another dog. Because of it he was not well liked among the other dog owners, but Kitty found him affecting.

Isaac was not as interested in the churchyard as Kitty was, perhaps because he didn't share her desire to be socially liberated. He liked playing with the dogs, but the conversations bored him. One evening when Isaac was with her, Kitty was talking with the owner of a mulish young basset hound, who mentioned that his dog wasn't housebroken. Kitty suggested crate training.

"It sounds mean but it's really not," she said. "The crate is supposed to be like a den, so they feel safe in there. First thing in the morning you take him right outside and give him a treat when he pees. You'd be surprised how quickly they get the idea."

"Tried it," the basset's owner said. "He stood in there rocking the crate back and forth till it tipped over, and then when

I opened the door, he ran upstairs and took a shit on my bed."

"The problem is," said Isaac, "your dog is an asshole. He needs to get over himself."

The bassett's owner was clearly offended. Isaac's world-view, in which a dog could be an asshole and could be called on it, was interesting to no one besides Kitty, so after a while she stopped trying to involve him in the society of the dog park.

At home, Mothra liked to keep Isaac company while he tinkered and experimented at his workbench in the basement. Isaac's workshop was a reliquary of antique hand tools and trash-picked chandeliers, lushly redolent of exotic solvents with names like naphtha, xylene, Japan drier. His basement stockpile was not, in fact, a pile but a collection from which he could always retrieve the correct size of cast iron hinge, or a certain shade of Minwax stain, or a Craftmatic bed motor, or an eight foot length of industrial roller track—or the electric-fence battery, which had been returned to its spot on the shelf until he could think of another use for it. Mothra found among Isaac's things a piece of egg crate foam and claimed it as her nest. Walking past the open door, Kitty heard snippets of one-sided conversation.

"Now watch how I mix up the paint. You have to make sure you get all the goo off the bottom of the can."

She imagined Mothra sitting at attention as he demonstrated, one ear standing up and the other bent forward at the tip.

The time came for Mothra to be spayed, but Isaac didn't see the need for it. "If she gets knocked up we can sell the puppies," he said.

It hadn't occurred to Kitty that she would have to mount a defense of something so obviously correct. Isaac answered all her arguments with apocalypto-nihilism. Overpopulation?

Fine, when they let me spay a few people I'll spay my dog. It was a retread of their fight over recycling: Isaac acknowledged the problem but he said Kitty was delusional if she thought she could do any good.

Kitty eventually won the fight through attrition: Isaac didn't stop her from making an appointment and taking her in. When she brought Mothra home from the vet, all weak and dopey, and settled her next to Isaac on their napping couch, Mothra rested her head on Isaac's lap while he stroked her belly, which had been shaved for the operation.

"This feels so weird," he said.

"I guess," Kitty said cautiously, detecting a note of exploratory zeal.

He was silent for a moment. "Wouldn't it be intense if her fur was all shaved like this?"

As high summer approached, Kitty and Mothra spent longer hours at the churchyard. On warm evenings, someone might show up with a case of beer. They would linger way past dinnertime and into the gathering dusk watching bats swoop around the giant old trees. Kitty looked forward to this time as much as Mothra did. Sometimes everyone stood around silently, watching the dogs. The puppies ran around in circles big and small, circles within circles, figure eights and zigzags. Some, like Mothra, were chasers, and some wanted to be chased. Mothra was far from the fastest, but she had a stock herder's instinct for the cutoff. The old dogs, the ones with white muzzles and cloudy eyes who were content to stand near their owners or sniff around the tree roots, filled Kitty with existential sadness. As with the people, Kitty found that her sympathies ranged wider and farther than she had ever imagined. She didn't, as she'd always thought, like the little bug-eyed dogs any less, or the fussy breed dogs with their strange haircuts. The delight of them, and the tragedy, was that they were as doggy as any others, bearing the yoke of human vanity with canine indifference.

The first real heat wave of the summer arrived, and the churchyard drew crowds of people avoiding the convective heat of their brick row houses. The dogs were lethargic and their owners cranky. Don was scrapping more and more with the others. He called one of the yuppies a fag and then refused to apologize. Everyone got involved. Kitty, who took it upon herself to smooth things over, learned that he was being evicted—along with Mandy, two cats, and a pet rat who shared his studio apartment with him. His disability case was headed to court, and soon he would be either homeless and broke or fifty thousand dollars richer. Kitty told him that maybe, in the meantime, he should switch from cocaine back to Vicodin if that was what it took for him to calm down a little.

There was no air conditioner in the house. The three of them—Isaac, Kitty, and Mothra—liked to sit outside on the cool marble stoop on hot afternoons. All up and down the block, people had the same idea. Radios played through open windows. Their neighbor ran a hose up from his basement through the sidewalk bulkhead and filled a kiddie pool. Children dragged their toys outside—Big Wheels, stuffed animals, tins of colored chalk.

Kitty balanced a bowl of green beans in her lap. She was snapping the ends off and dropping them into a pot on the step next to her.

"I'm going for a six-pack," Isaac said. "C'mon, Mothra."

"Leash." Kitty snapped it to Mothra's collar and handed the end to Isaac.

Isaac took Mothra's leash off as soon as they rounded the corner. They ducked into Costello's. Mothra lay at the foot of Isaac's stool while he drank a short glass of beer at the bar, her ears and fur riffling in the breeze from the industrial floor fan. The Brylcreemed bartender handed a pot of water over the counter without comment, and Isaac set it down next to her. She lifted her head in acknowledgement, then flopped back on the cool tiles.

Walking out of the bar half an hour later with the six-pack in a paper bag, they surprised two small boys on the sidewalk, who shrieked and hugged the wall as they passed.

"Wolf! Wolf!" yelled the older boy.

Isaac snorted. "That's right!" He and Mothra exchanged a sly glance and headed home. "She wouldn't be so hot if you let me shave her fur," he said to Kitty when they got to the stoop.

"No, Isaac!"

Kitty woke early the next morning to the bounce of Mothra jumping onto the bed. Shielding her eyes against a harsh slant of sunlight, she reached over and felt not fur but stubble. Dropping her other hand, she saw that everything but Mothra's head and her paws had been clipped down to the blue-black skin. Her tail thumped hairlessly on the bed. Kitty ran downstairs and found Isaac in the bathroom, electric clipper in hand, standing in a pile of lustrous black fur. He smiled when he saw her.

"What the hell is wrong with you?"

"She was hot," he said, suddenly glum.

Kitty learned that dogs can get sunburns. Mothra had to wear a T-shirt when she went outside, which delighted the neighborhood kids but made Kitty prickle with humiliation. Under the shirt her skin chafed and flaked and erupted in a rash. In the waiting room at the vet's office, a nice lady with a cat carrier on her lap asked Kitty what happened, and when Kitty explained, she said, "I hope you showed that fellow the door!"

But Kitty did not show Isaac the door. She even found herself in the position of defending him at the churchyard.

"If someone did that to Mandy, I'd kick his ass," Don said.

The basset owner tried to convince Kitty that Isaac was dangerous. "They always start out on animals," he said. "Gary Heidnik, Jeffrey Dahmer. Look it up."

"No," said Kitty, "he's not a sadist. He's just got an overactive imagination."

"What's imaginative about shaving a dog?"

This was hard to explain. What she was thinking of was a kind of ecstatic tunnel vision, peculiar to Isaac. Once the possibility of the shaved dog had found its way into in his brain, she'd been unable to dislodge it. Now she tried to at least make him see why it troubled her, what he had done. They argued in circles. He admitted that he'd been curious about seeing Mothra without her fur, but he always came back to the same position: it was hot, and therefore, whatever caused the initial impulse, he was justified in shaving her. Anyhow, dogs got haircuts all the time, and Kitty was making way too big a deal of the whole thing.

Mothra wasn't angry. She still kept Isaac company in the basement and took naps with him. After all, she'd stood cooperatively for the entire twenty or thirty minutes it took him to buzz off her fur, and if she had any misgivings about the results she forgot them instantly, because that was the way of dogs.

Kitty, on the other hand, couldn't seem to let it go. Every time she looked at Mothra she found herself un-forgiving Isaac a bit more.

"I think I get it," said he one day. "It's like when I was five, and I took my parents' alarm clock apart, and no one could figure out how to put it back together, and then they had to throw it out and buy a new one."

"No," Kitty said, "It's nothing like that. Your parents' clock was not *sentient*. This is the whole problem, this right here."

"Don't worry," he said, rolling his eyes. "I learned my lesson."

"What lesson?"

"Don't shave the dog."

"I'm not just trying to be right, you know," Kitty said. "It really bothers me that you haven't learned anything from this."

"Fine. If we ever get a cat, I won't shave that either."

"I can't believe you're still joking about this."

"You know what I can't believe? I can't believe you're still bitching about it. Jesus Christ, get over it, Kitty. The dog is fine. Aren't you fine, Mothra?" The dog, who had been lying on the floor shifting her eyes from Isaac to Kitty and back again, perked up at the sound of her name. "Anyhow," he continued, "who bought her? Me. I bought her, she's my dog, so fuck off."

Kitty took all the money in her pocket and threw it at him. "You want your thirty dollars? *Here.*"

"No sale."

Isaac and Mothra were driving through the utilitarian drear of Northeast Philly looking for a floor supply warehouse. It was here somewhere, in one of these shitty industrial parks. While Isaac was scanning the parking lot signs on the side of the road, he noticed someone scuttling along the ditch with a red plastic gas can. Short, scrawny, frizzy grey hair. He looked familiar. Oh yeah, that guy from the dog park—Kitty's wasteoid friend. He pulled alongside the guy and rolled down the passenger side window.

"Hey, I know you," he yelled.

Don didn't immediately recognize Isaac. He walked over and leaned in the window.

"Hey, uh . . ."

"Isaac."

"Yeah, right—Isaac, Isaac," said Don.

"What are you doing walking around out here?"

Don waved his gas can.

"Let me give you a lift," Isaac said. He reached across and opened the door.

"Man, I'm glad you stopped," said Don, sliding in. He leaned over the seat to put the gas can in the back and Mothra stood up to say hello. "Hey, lookit you." Don gave her neck a scruff. "Her fur's growing back. Is she gonna be grey like this now?"

"I think that's just her undercoat."

"I gotta say, she looks a lot better with a little fluff."

Isaac ignored it.

"I mean, she looked pretty fucking weird," Don added.

"I guess."

"Like a plucked chicken or something."

"Yeah yeah yeah. I thought I'd never hear the end of that one."

"Kitty's a nice girl, man. My old girlfriend would've kicked my ass if I pulled a stunt like that."

"I know," Isaac said with a sigh. "She's a class act."

They filled the gas can at a Sunoco and headed back toward Don's car. Isaac turned on the car radio and found the Drexel station.

"Oh yeah," said Don approvingly when a Dictators song came on.

"Hey Don, are you a musician?" Isaac asked.

"No, why?"

"You look like Handsome Dick Manitoba. Did anyone ever tell you that?"

"Really?" said Don, pleased. "You really think so?

"I guess it's the hair."

By the time they got back to Don's car, they were having such a nice time chatting about this and that—punk rock,

Don's settlement check and how to spend it—that they decided to pick up a six-pack and drive around some more. Enjoy the sunset. The check was coming in any day, and Don was going to take Kitty's advice. He was going to buy a little row house, maybe somewhere down near Packer Park where the prices were still low. He was living in a motel in South Jersey right now. He'd had to get rid of the cats, which broke his heart. But at least he still had his rat, and of course Mandy, and soon they'd have their own little place. Kitty and Isaac could come over sometimes, and bring Mothra.

"Tell you what," said Don after a while, "I have a little bit of coke here. You want to pull in somewhere and do a line? Just don't tell Kitty, okay?"

Isaac hesitated. "I don't really like coke."

"I have a joint . . ."

"I can't smoke weed either."

"What *do* you like?"

Isaac thought for a minute. He liked acid, but that was probably out of the question. "Heroin. I like heroin."

"Well, why didn't you say so?" Don said. "Turn around."

They headed back south. Mothra sat up in the back seat and watched the drive-thrus and car lots and clusters of vinyl-clad row houses roll past in the growing darkness. Soon they were traveling under the Frankford El, through the dollar store corridor of Juniata, and into the nefarious Kensington gloom. They stopped outside a bar with a glass brick front. Don went in and came outside with a guy in a do-rag and an enormous white t-shirt. The two disappeared around the corner. Don came back a few minutes later, alone. He got in the front seat and handed Isaac a glassine bindle. It had a little skull and crossbones and the word FLATLINE stamped on it.

"That's the high-test," said Don. "So, you're not gonna tell Kitty about this, right?" He pulled something else out of his pocket: a needle. Isaac hadn't thought of that, but what the hell.

It was high-test, all right. Isaac woke up on the ground in the lot behind the glass brick bar with a flashlight shining in his eyes and a shot of Narcan in his arm. He was suddenly not high at all, and Don was nowhere. The scenery sloshed past as the paramedics rolled him onto a gurney: a urine-streaked wall, a shot-out street light, a row of houses across the street staring back at him with distempered plywood eyes. As they lifted Isaac into the ambulance, he saw that the front doors of his car were wide open.

"Mothra," he said, or had he only thought it?

the_lettuce

Kitty met Isaac a few weeks after her thirtieth birthday and stayed with him for eleven years. He was gloomy and angry, chronically disorganized, estranged from his family. A few years into their relationship, when she realized how dependent he'd become on her, Kitty considered leaving, but she didn't. Maybe this was just adult life, she told herself, this feeling of entanglement. It wasn't easy living with someone; everyone said so. Instead of breaking up, they bought a run-down row house in South Philadelphia and worked on it together over the years, never quite getting it past the construction-site stage.

And Isaac never stopped being exhausting. He wrecked her car and picked fights with the neighbors and followed her around the house ranting about the housewives who hired him to install kitchen cabinets and refinish their floors. Increasingly, Kitty found herself asking, "What if this is *not* adult life?" If it wasn't, she was running out of time. It was already, practically speaking, too late for children—not that she had ever actively wanted them; Isaac was enough. In the end, she picked a moment when they weren't fighting and took him to the diner across the street to tell him, over hamburgers, that she couldn't be with him anymore. She was moving into the spare room. He didn't ask for an explanation. He seemed to have been expecting it.

They kept living together as roommates, waiting out the bad real estate market. She didn't do his laundry anymore, but they ate dinner in front of the TV several nights a week. Once, they watched a movie about a strange, religiously ecstatic young bride in a backward Scottish village. In the movie, her husband is paralyzed in an oil rig accident. She believes God has punished them for their carnal happiness. Her husband tells her to sleep with other men and describe their encounters for him, which she does, and in her strangeness and simplicity, she becomes convinced that she is keeping him alive in this way. As his health fails, her assignations become more desperate. She ends up battered and ruined, and she dies in disgrace, denied a church funeral.

Kitty thought it was the saddest movie she'd ever seen. She and Isaac were both crying by the time the credits rolled, and they ended up together in their old bed. When she woke up in the middle of the night, his arms were clamped around her waist. She pried herself free and went back to the spare room. In the morning he tried to kiss her when she poured him a cup of coffee, but she turned her head away and said, "I'm sorry."

Kitty had no idea how a forty-one-year-old was supposed to meet someone new. Before she moved in with Isaac, her social universe had seemed to contain infinite romantic permutations. She'd worked in crowded places—a coffee shop, a bookstore, a rock club—wandering in and out of flirtations and affairs; but the crowds were gone now. No one called on Friday to tell her where the weekend's parties were, and if she did find herself at a party, it was no longer a labyrinth of erotic possibilities.

Someone at work told her about a free online dating website called cupid.com.

"You're not really going to do this, are you?" her friend Nancy asked when she brought it up.

"Sure, why not? Aren't you curious?"

"So, you put up an ad? Like an escort?"

"Not exactly. You create a profile, a little homunculus, and you give it all your essential qualities so that it can attract appropriate suitors while you are busy beach-walking, reading great books, feeling equally at home in sweatpants or an evening gown."

Ironic distance made the idea more bearable. Kitty chose the name "foam_core" for her online identity and uploaded a picture of herself wearing a heavy winter coat and rubber boots. Then she turned to the lifestyle questionnaire. Most of the questions were optional, designed for a balance of sincerity and display.

*In my bedroom you will find*___. She skipped that one.

___ *is sexy; ___ is sexier.* Skip.

Five things I can't live without; 25 years from now I see myself; The last thing that made me laugh out loud was. She left these blank as well.

The door slammed downstairs. "Hey," she yelled to Isaac. "How would you describe me in one word?"

"Crabby."

The only two questions you had to answer were *Why You Should Get To Know Me* and *What I'm Looking For.* She could not think of a way to address the first one without sounding like an asshole. The second one, though, uncorked a stream.

"Reclusive geniuses," she wrote. "Hyperactive lunatics, charismatic vulgarians, obsessive motor-mouths." Lists were her favorite mode of self-expression. "Collectors of arcane knowledge and useless ephemera." She typed without pausing for a while, then reviewed what she had written. She added, "You can be a kook as long as you're an interesting kook, and I don't care if you have a high school diploma."

Her cupid.com mailbox began filling up, but the men who wrote to her comprised a different sort of list. They were U2 fans and jet-skiers, sad-eyed home-brewers and readers of medical thrillers. She was considering deactivating her account when she got a message from "expunk63," a video editor who liked Flipper and Black Flag. He was the first person she'd encountered who seemed like someone she might know socially, in real life, so she agreed to meet him at a bar in Old City.

The evening was a traumatic failure. In person, expunk63 was combative and jittery. She'd forgotten the agony of first-date small talk.

"What do you edit," she asked. "Movies? TV?"

"Documentaries."

She said she liked Werner Herzog's documentaries. "You mean you like *Grizzly Man*," he said. "You've probably never even heard of *Fata Morgana*. You don't understand Herzog if you haven't seen that."

She took a long break after expunk63, but eventually she went back to the website. She went out with an improv comic and a goateed architecture student and even a Wharton professor, whom she dated twice, mostly because she was so surprised he asked her out again. On their second date she mentioned her roommate situation, and when she got home she found an e-mail from him outlining the life actions she would have to agree to if they were to continue seeing each other—number one on the list being a complete financial separation from Isaac.

The biggest surprise was how many men only seemed interested in writing back and forth. They would suggest moving from cupid.com over to their regular e-mail addresses, and then they'd draw out the correspondence for days and sometimes weeks, strafing her with questions about her family, pets, and food preferences, asking her for lists of her favorite records and movies and supplying their own. Some probed her for increasingly intimate details about her romantic history. As long as the guy was kooky and interesting enough, she'd keep answering questions. She didn't want to seem like a prude, and, frankly, she enjoyed the attention. A few managed to get her to supply enough anatomical details (nipple extension, areola color, pubic styling) to produce customized smut. But these men, who were happy to send her pictures of their erections, would vanish when she pressed them for live meetings.

After a while, she decided not to give out her real e-mail address to anyone until she'd met him in person. To simplify things and cut back on all the pre-screening—which had not proved to be particularly effective in any case—she began suggesting a get-together with anyone she hadn't ruled out after a few exchanges on cupid.com. And so it was that, within a few months, the ironic distance was obliterated, and her romantic prospects had been downgraded to a string of unpromising afternoon coffee dates.

Kitty sat down at her desk with the day's mail: a letter from her mother, a postcard from the dentist, and something addressed to Isaac from the DMV. She put them aside and checked her e-mail and, out of habit, logged onto cupid.com. There was a new message from someone calling himself "the_lettuce."

"Hi, foam_core. That is a funny name. Why did you choose it, I wonder? My real name is Eric. I guess my picture is kind of small. I don't know if I am any of those things you mentioned, charismatic and genius and all those. I don't think I'm vulgar either, but I couldn't tell if you were joking about that one. Anyhow I wanted to say hi and that you seem like a very unique person."

His picture was small. It only expanded on her screen to the size of a business card. He appeared to be hiking in the mountains, wearing a floppy outdoorsman-type hat that suggested baldness. He was shading his eyes with his left hand and squinting in a way that distorted his whole face. She clicked through to his profile and saw nothing that stood out.

"Hi, Eric. Kitty here. I don't know why I called myself foam_core. It just popped into my head. What about you? Why are you the_lettuce? I live pretty close to Center City. Where are you?"

She turned back to the letter from the DMV. It looked bad. It was from the Office of Finance. When they were together, Kitty had opened all Isaac's official-looking mail—not because she was a snoop, but because he expected it of her. "You're like an extra lobe of my brain," he'd said to her once. For her part, she'd have loved to spare herself knowing about his missed credit card payments and unpaid parking tickets, but she'd learned that if she didn't open his mail it would keep piling up until some disaster occurred. He would miss an important payment or a filing date or a court appearance. His checking account would be closed or his health insurance would be canceled or some massive fine would accrue. In the end, dealing with his self-pity and rage took more out of her than just staying top of his mail. But it was not her job anymore. She put the envelope down, and then picked it up again. The words "FINAL NOTICE" were stamped in red across the front.

"Fuck me," she said, tearing it open.

The letter, covered in official seals, said that the registration for his work van had been suspended for six months: a penalty for letting his insurance lapse. When she looked up, there was already a response from the_lettuce.

"Hi, Kitty. Thanks for writing back. I chose that name, the_lettuce, two years ago when I signed up. Back then I was the produce manager at a natural food store in Ardmore, which is where I live."

Kitty was a few minutes late for her coffee date with the_lettuce. In her mind he was still the_lettuce, not Eric. She had a hard time thinking of her Internet dates by their real names, even after she'd met them. She'd been running around all morning dealing with Isaac's van; she'd spent several hours at the DMV putting the registration in her own name and then taken it for a safety-and-smog inspection. She disliked driving the van, especially here on the Main Line, because of all Isaac's horrible homemade bumper stickers. "Killing Arabs = Jobs," "We Bomb Because We Care," "God Hates You and Your Family," half a dozen others—many of them frayed around the edges where people had tried to tear them off. How, she wondered, did he manage to drive around without getting pulled over for every rolling stop and illegal right on red—or for that matter, without being punched out by a Marine for his upside-down American flag decal? She backed into a spot in the Starbucks parking lot.

the_lettuce was already there, sitting at a corner table, wearing a short-sleeved tropical print shirt, as he'd told her he would be. He was bent forward, scribbling on a pad of paper, and didn't see Kitty approach.

"Eric?"

He looked up, momentarily startled. He was indeed bald but for an almost-invisible crescent of gingery hair. His eyes were pale and lashless behind wire-rimmed glasses, and his neck, arms, and what showed of his chest were covered with a bright rash.

"Kitty?" He stood up. He was wearing shorts—khakis with pleats across the front. She felt an immediate and desperate need to put him at ease.

"I'm going to get myself something to drink," she said. "Don't go anywhere, okay?"

When she sat down with her tea, she saw that he was working on a pad of graph paper. He'd been filling in the quarter-inch squares with a rapidograph pen. "What's that?" she asked.

"Oh." He flushed, so that his cheeks matched his inflamed neck. "It's just this thing I do. Kind of— it's like drawing, I guess. I have an algorithm. See?" He opened his left hand and showed her a pair of dice. "I roll them, and depending on what numbers come up, I fill in the square, or half the square, or I just draw a dot in it, or I leave it blank. Then I move to the next square and roll the dice again." He pulled a loose sheet out of his pad and presented it to her. It was covered from edge to edge with markings, so densely inked that it felt a little heavy. She stared for a minute, as though it were one of those magic eye paintings, hoping to find some kind of pattern, but none emerged.

"Well, I've never seen anything like it," she said, handing it back. "How long have you been making these?"

"I don't know. I guess since I was a kid."

"Do you make any other kind of art? Painting? Or . . . regular drawings?"

"No, just this. This is it." He massaged the dice in his left hand.

Kitty searched for a follow-up question. How had they managed to find their way into this conversational cul-de-sac so quickly? "So," she said, "you said you worked at a health food store?"

"No. I mean, yes, but not anymore. I worked at the Nature Mart for almost twenty years, but they changed management last year and I lost my job."

"Oh, I *am* sorry."

"Well, at first they offered to let me stay, but I would have been back to cashier. And then they changed their mind anyhow. I probably would have stayed if they hadn't changed their mind."

"Gee."

"I'm sorry. I don't know why I'm telling you this."

"It's okay."

Kitty drank her tea, and then another tea. She learned that, since losing his job at Nature Mart, the_lettuce been working at Dover Pneumatics, a company that manufactured and distributed door closure units. His younger brother had hired him, reluctantly and under family pressure, and had from the beginning been submitting him to subtle forms of humiliation—like ignoring his request for a bathroom key and not telling him about sales meetings and, just last week, having his desk moved into a hallway. Other than the graph paper drawings, his only hobby was playing Go. He'd participated in some children's tournaments and done badly. He lived in an apartment with his best friend from high school, who was on disability and spent weeks at a time on the couch in his bathrobe and slippers. They had nothing in common anymore. It had at least been convenient when the_lettuce still worked at the health food store, but he didn't drive, and now he had to get up while it was still dark to take SEPTA into town, and then another train to Delaware. His brother had already written him up several times for being late to work, and he'd been docked some vacation days. He massaged the dice in his left hand while he told her all this. It seemed to calm him.

"Have you thought about moving?" Kitty asked.

"I'm waiting until my cat dies." His cat had feline leukemia and wasn't expected to live much longer but was, he said, very attached to the roommate.

A sunbeam that had been inching along the wall reached their corner, and the_lettuce held his left hand over his eyes and squinted: a tableau vivant of his tiny profile picture. Kitty noticed that his rash had faded to a light pink. When she looked at her watch, she saw that he had been talking for over an hour, but the effect, somehow, was not alienating. She'd made suggestions here and there, but mainly, she sensed, he needed her to bear witness. This was something she could do.

"Thank you," he said. "I mean, thank you for suggesting this."

"Thank you for coming."

"I mean it. I've been on cupid.com for two years, and you're the first person who ever asked me on a . . ." He trailed off, unable to say the word.

"Did *you* ever ask anyone? On a date? On the site, I mean."

He shook his head.

"Eric, are you lonely?"

"Aren't you?"

"Well, yes, I suppose." She thought of Isaac, though, and realized that it wasn't true. "Can I ask you something else?"

"Please."

"When was the last time you had a girlfriend?"

"It's been a long time. A long time."

"What about sex?" The words came out before she considered them, but he didn't seem embarrassed.

"It's been over ten years," he said.

"Ten years?"

"*Over* ten years." His expression was frank and his tone affectless, as though he were describing a chronic pain to which he'd grown accustomed.

"This is going to sound weird," she said, "and I really hope you don't take it the wrong way, and you don't have to answer if you don't want to."

"No, go ahead."

"Did you ever think about paying someone?"

"I did think of that, yes, many times. But I couldn't go through with it."

Kitty imagined the_lettuce turning to the ads in the back of the *City Paper*, picking up his phone and then putting it down again. She needed a moment to get her bearings. "Eric," she said, "will you excuse me?

186

The bathroom smelled of dried eucalyptus and Glade air freshener. The walls were stippled with peach-colored sponge paint. Kitty splashed her face in the sink and looked at herself in the mirror. There had never been a labyrinth of erotic possibilities for the_lettuce—not ten years ago, not even twenty. She was certain of that. She dug around in her pocketbook. In a zippered pocket hidden in the lining, she found it: a blue foil packet she'd been carrying around since that first hopeful date with expunk63.

Only when the_lettuce was sitting in the passenger seat of Isaac's van did it occur to Kitty that she would have to seduce him. At first, he'd declined her offer of a ride. But she'd insisted, and now here he was, nervously toggling the switch for the electric window.

"Turn here," he said. "Right." They descended a hill that went past the Ardmore SEPTA station.

"Are you in a hurry to get home? I'd like to pull over for a bit."

"You want to pull over?"

She turned into the station and parked at the far end of the lot, where there were no other cars. They sat silently for a moment, looking out the windshield at a row of dusty sumac bushes.

"I kind of figured I wouldn't see you again," he said.

"Can I be honest? I don't think you will."

"I didn't expect it. You don't have to explain."

"No, that's not what I mean. That's not why I wanted to stop here." She turned in her seat to look at him. A delicate nimbus of late afternoon light surrounded his large head and narrow shoulders. She unbuckled her seatbelt, moving slowly and carefully, as she would around a skittish animal. "I'm going to come over there," she said. "Okay? I'm coming over to you now."

He took off his glasses and looked at her with large, grave eyes while she undid his seatbelt and lowered herself onto his lap, resting her knees on the seat on either side of him. She saw now that he wasn't lashless: his eyelashes were almost translucent, but they were long and gently curled. She kissed him, and he kissed her back tentatively. His breath tasted of the coffee he'd nursed for the entire hour they had spent at Starbucks. She could feel his heart beating beneath his tropical shirt. Pressing into his lap, she felt a slight movement in response, but his arms stayed at his sides.

"These angles won't work," she said. "Let me make some space in back."

He stayed up front while she moved Isaac's shop vac to one side, and his tool cases, and the milk crates full of sanding disks, and the boxes of nail cartridges. She found a heavy furniture pad and shook the sawdust out the side door, then spread it out in the space she'd cleared. "Okay," she said, peeling her T-shirt off. "Do you want to come back?"

She kneeled in her bra and panties and looked up at him while he undressed. He was very thin, covered everywhere with fine, reddish-blond hair. She reached for his hand and pulled him down next to her, and they lay side by side kissing. Sucking his lower lip to stop his hard little tongue from darting around in her mouth, she felt him relax. She guided his hand inside her panties, willing herself to think of him, the_lettuce, Eric, and no one else as the light dimmed, softening the outlines of the tool cases and crates around them.

"Thank you," he said over and over as they made love. At first she shushed him, but she felt it too: gratitude. After a while, his words became sighs.

Kitty waited at the curb while the_lettuce unlocked the door to his apartment. He looked like a little kid with his backpack and short pants. He turned and waved, and she waved back until he was inside. The light came on in the living room and a cat jumped up on the windowsill—the one with feline leukemia, she supposed. She did a three-point turn in the wide street and drove past the train station. The lot was empty now.

Kitty thought of the strange movie about the Scottish fishing village—the one that made her and Isaac cry. At a stoplight on Montgomery Ave she dug her cell phone out of her pocketbook, but then she remembered the bumper stickers. Best not to risk a ticket. She pulled up to a meter and put the van in park. She considered whether to tell Isaac about the_lettuce. After all, they were nothing like that couple. Isaac wasn't paralyzed and she wasn't a young bride.

While she dialed Isaac's number, she pictured the_lettuce shrugging off his backpack, pouring himself a glass of milk, uncapping his rapidograph pen at the kitchen table. She wondered if he would move to Delaware. She hoped not. She didn't know what she did hope for him, but not that.

ACKNOWLEDGMENTS

First thanks go to Mike McGonigal and Steve Connell, and to Caleb Rochester for being my muse and my buddy. Thanks also to Leslie Epstein, Sigrid Nunez, Xuefei Jin, David Brainard, Soo Yeon Hong, Joy Harris, Bonnie Jo Campbell, James Parker, and Peter Doyle for their advice and moral support; to Jenny Davidson, Katya Apekina, and Mairead Case for their help with the manuscript; and to the Ucross Foundation, the Virginia Center for the Creative Arts, and the membership of one or more secret cabals. Most of all, I am grateful to my mother, Joanna Herlihy; my siblings, Sonia, Nate, and Sam; and my first literary role model: my father, the late, great Alexander Lipson.

CPSIA information can be obtained at www.ICGtesting.com
Printed in the USA
LVOW06s1138080414

380818LV00001B/1/P